Back by Popular Demand

A collector's edition of favorite titles from one of the world's best-loved romance authors. Harlequin is proud to bring back these sought-after titles and present them as one cherished collection.

BETTY NEELS: COLLECTOR'S EDITION

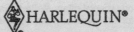

HARLEQUIN®

Betty Neels spent her childhood and youth in Devonshire before training as a nurse and midwife. She was an army nursing sister during the war, married a Dutchman and subsequently lived in Holland for fourteen years. She now lives with her husband in Dorset, and has a daughter and grandson. Her hobbies are reading, animals, old buildings and, of course, writing. Betty started to write on retirement from nursing, incited by a lady in a library bemoaning the lack of romantic novels.

Mrs. Neels is always delighted to receive fan letters, but would truly appreciate it if they could be directed to Harlequin Mills & Boon Ltd., 18-24 Paradise Road, Richmond, Surrey, TW9 1SR, England.

Books by Betty Neels

Don't miss any of our special offers. Write to us at the following address for information on our newest releases.

Harlequin Reader Service
U.S.: 3010 Walden Ave., P.O. Box 1325, Buffalo, NY 14269
Canadian: P.O. Box 609, Fort Erie, Ont. L2A 5X3

BETTY NEELS

RING IN A TEACUP

COLLECTOR'S EDITION

HARLEQUIN®

TORONTO • NEW YORK • LONDON
AMSTERDAM • PARIS • SYDNEY • HAMBURG
STOCKHOLM • ATHENS • TOKYO • MILAN • MADRID
PRAGUE • WARSAW • BUDAPEST • AUCKLAND

ISBN 0-373-63102-2

RING IN A TEACUP

First North American Publication 1999.

Copyright © 1978 by Betty Neels.

Visit us at www.romance.net

Printed in U.S.A.

CHAPTER ONE

THE SUN, already warmer than it should have been for nine o'clock on an August morning, poured through the high, uncurtained windows of the lecture hall at St Norbert's Hospital, highlighting the rows of uniformed figures, sitting according to status, their differently coloured uniform dresses making a cheerful splash of colour against the drab paintwork, their white caps constantly bobbing to and fro as they enjoyed a good gossip before their lecture began—all but the two front rows; the night nurses sat there, silently resentful of having to attend a lecture when they should have been on their way to hot baths, unending cups of tea, yesterday's paper kindly saved by a patient, and finally, blissful bed.

And in the middle of the front row sat student nurse Lucy Prendergast, a small slip of a girl, with mousy hair, pleasing though not pretty features and enormous green eyes, her one claim to beauty. But as she happened to be fast asleep, their devastating glory wasn't in evidence, indeed she looked downright plain; a night of non-stop work on Children's had done nothing to improve her looks.

She would probably have gone on sleeping, sitting

bolt upright on her hard chair, if her neighbours hadn't dug her in the ribs and begged her to stir herself as a small procession of Senior Sister Tutor, her two assistants and a clerk to make notes, trod firmly across the platform and seated themselves and a moment later, nicely timed, the lecturer, whose profound utterances the night nurses had been kept from their beds to hear, came in.

There was an immediate hush and then a gentle sigh from the rows of upturned faces; it had been taken for granted that he would be elderly, pompous, bald, and mumbling, but he was none of these things—he was very tall, extremely broad, and possessed of the kind of good looks so often written about and so seldom seen; moreover he was exquisitely dressed and when he replied to their concerted 'good morning, sir,' his voice was deep, slow and made all the more interesting by reason of its slight foreign accent.

His audience, settling in their seats, sat back to drink in every word and take a good look at him at the same time—all except Nurse Prendergast, who hadn't even bothered to open her eyes properly. True, she had risen to her feet when everyone else did, because her good friends on either side of her had dragged her to them, but seated again she dropped off at once and continued to sleep peacefully throughout the lecture, unheeding of the deep voice just above her head, explaining all the finer points of angiitis obliterans and its treatment, and her friends, sharing the quite erroneous idea that the occupants of the first two rows were quite safe from the eyes of the lecturer on the platform, for they believed that he always looked above their heads into the body of the hall, allowed her to sleep on. Everything would have been just fine if he hadn't started asking questions, picking members of his audience at random. When he asked: 'And the result of these tests would be...' his eyes, roaming along the rows of attentive faces before him, came to rest upon Lucy's gently nodding head.

A ferocious gleam came into his eyes; she could have been looking down into her lap, but he was willing to bet with himself that she wasn't.

'The nurse in the centre of the first row,' he added softly.

Lucy, dug savagely in the ribs by her nervous friends, opened her eyes wide and looked straight at him. She was bemused by sleep and had no idea what he had said or what she was supposed to say herself. She stared up at the handsome, bland face above her; she had never seen eyes glitter, but the cold blue ones boring into hers were glittering all right. A wash of bright pink crept slowly over her tired face, but it was a flush of temper rather than a blush of shame; she was peevish from lack of sleep and her resentment was stronger than anything else just at that moment. She said in a clear, controlled voice: 'I didn't hear what you were saying, sir—I was asleep.'

His expression didn't alter, although she had the feeling that he was laughing silently. She added politely, 'I'm sorry, sir,' and sighed with relief as his gaze swept over her head to be caught and held by the eager efforts of a girl Lucy couldn't stand at any price—Martha Inskip, the know-all of her set; always ready with the right answers to Sister Tutor's questions, always the one to get the highest marks in written papers, and yet quite incapable of making a patient comfortable in bed— The lecturer said almost wearily: 'Yes, Nurse?' and then listened impassively to her perfect answer to the question Lucy had so regrettably not heard.

He asked more questions after that, but never once did he glance at Lucy, wide awake now and brooding unhappily about Sister Tutor's reactions. Reactions which reared their ugly heads as the lecture came to a close with the formal leavetaking of the lecturer as he stalked off the platform with Sister Tutor and her attendants trailing him. Her severe back was barely out of sight before the orderly lines of nurses broke up into groups and began to make their way back to their various destinations. Lucy was well down the corridor leading to the maze of passages which would take her to the Nurses' Home when a breathless nurse caught up with her. 'Sister Tutor wants you,' she said urgently, 'in the ante-room.'

Lucy didn't say a word; she had been pushing her luck and now there was nothing to do about it; she hadn't really believed that she would get off scot free. She crossed the lecture hall and went through the door by the platform into the little room used by the lecturers. There were only two people in it, Sister Tutor and the lecturer, and the former said at once in a voice which held disapproval: 'I will leave you to apologise to Doctor der Linssen, Nurse Prendergast,' and sailed out of the room.

The doctor stood where he was, looking at her. Presently he asked: 'Your name is Prendergast?' and when she nodded: 'A peculiar name.' Which so incensed her that she said snappily: 'I did say I was sorry.'

'Oh, yes, indeed. Rest assured that it was not I who insisted on you returning.'

He looked irritable and tired. She said kindly: 'I expect your pride's hurt, but it doesn't need to be; everyone thought you were smashing, and I would have gone to sleep even if you'd been Michael Caine or Kojak.'

A kind of spasm shook the doctor's patrician features, but he said merely: 'You are on night duty, Miss—er—Prendergast.' It wasn't a question.

'Yes. The children's ward—always so busy and just unspeakable last night, and then I had a huge breakfast and it's fatal to sit down afterwards,' and when he made no reply added in a motherly way: 'I expect you're quite nice at home with your wife and children.'

'I have not as yet either wife or children.' He sounded outraged. 'You speak as though you were a securely married mother of a large family. Are you married, Miss Prendergast?'

'Me? no—I'd be Mrs if I were, and who'd want to marry me? But I've got brothers and sisters, and we had such fun when we were children.'

His voice was icy. 'You lack respect, young lady, and you are impertinent. You should not be nursing, you should be one of those interfering females who go around telling other people how to lead their lives and assuring them that happiness is just around the corner.'

She tried not to blush, but she couldn't stop herself; she was engulfed in a red glow, but she looked him in the eye. 'I don't blame you for getting your own back,' she added a sir this time. 'Now we're equal, aren't we?'

She didn't wait to be dismissed but flew through the door as though she had the devil at her heels, back the way she had come, almost bursting with rage and dislike of him; it took several cups of tea and half an hour in a very hot bath reading the *Daily Mirror* before she was sufficiently calmed down to go to bed and sleep at last.

Lucy forgot the whole regrettable business in no time at all; she was rushed off her feet on duty and

when she was free she slept soundly like the healthy
girl she was, and if, just once or twice, she remembered the good-looking lecturer, she pushed him to
the back of her mind; she was no daydreamer—besides, he hadn't liked her.

She had expected a lecture from Sister Tutor, but
no word had been said; probably, thought Lucy, she
considered that she had been sufficiently rebuked for
her behaviour.

She went home for her nights off at the end of the
following week, a quite long journey which she
could only afford once a month. The small village
outside Beaminster, which wasn't much more than a
village itself, was buried in the Dorset hills; it meant
going by train to Crewkerne where she was met by
her father, Rector of Dedminster and the hamlets of
Lodcombe and Twistover, in the shaky old Ford used
by every member of the family if they happened to
be at home.

Her father met her at the station, an elderly man
with mild blue eyes who had passed on his very ordinary features to her; except for the green eyes, of
course, and no one in the family knew where they
had come from. He led her out to the car, and after
a good deal of poking around coaxed it to start, but
once they were bowling sedately towards Beaminster, he embarked on a gentle dissertation about the
parish, the delightful weather and the various odds

and ends of news about her mother and brothers and sisters.

Lucy listened with pleasure; he was so restful after the rush and hurry of hospital life, and he was so kind. She had a fleeting memory of the lecturer, who hadn't been kind at all, and then shook her head angrily to get rid of his image, with its handsome features and pale hair.

The Rectory was a large rambling place, very inconvenient; all passages and odd stairs and small rooms leading from the enormous kitchen, which in an earlier time must have housed a horde of servants. Lucy darted through the back door and found her mother at the kitchen table, hulling strawberries—a beautiful woman still, even with five grown-up children, four of whom had inherited her striking good looks, leaving Lucy to be the plain one in the family, although as her mother pointed out often enough, no one else had emerald green eyes.

Lucy perched on the table and gobbled up strawberries while she answered her mother's questions; they were usually the same, only couched in carefully disguised ways: had Lucy met any nice young men? had she been out? and if by some small chance she had, the young man had to be described down to the last coat button, even though Lucy pointed out that in most cases he was already engaged or had merely asked her out in order to pave the way to an introduction to one of her friends. She had little to tell this time; she was going to save the lecturer for later.

'Lovely to be home,' she observed contentedly. 'Who's here?'

'Kitty and Jerry and Paul, dear. Emma's got her hands full with the twins—they've got the measles.'

Emma was the eldest and married, and both her brothers were engaged, while Kitty was the very new wife of a BOAC pilot, on a visit while he went on a course.

'Good,' said Lucy. 'What's for dinner?'

Her parent gave her a loving look; Lucy, so small and slim, had the appetite of a large horse and never put on an ounce.

'Roast beef, darling, and it's almost ready.'

It was over Mrs Prendergast's splendidly cooked meal that Lucy told them all about her unfortunate lapse during the lecture.

'Was he good-looking?' Kitty wanted to know.

'Oh, very, and very large too—not just tall but wide as well; he towered, if you know what I mean, and cold blue eyes that looked through me and the sort of hair that could be either very fair or grey.' She paused to consider. 'Oh, and he had one of those deep, rather gritty voices.'

Her mother, portioning out trifle, gave her a quick glance. 'But you didn't like him, love?'

Lucy, strictly brought up as behoved a parson's

daughter, answered truthfully and without embarrassment.

'Well, actually, I did—he was smashing. Now if it had been Kitty or Emma...they'd have known what to do, and anyway, he wouldn't have minded them; they're both so pretty.' She sighed. 'But he didn't like me, and why should he, for heaven's sake? Snoring through his rolling periods!'

'Looks are not everything, Lucilla,' observed her father mildly, who hadn't really been listening and had only caught the bit about being pretty. 'Perhaps a suitable regret for your rudeness in falling asleep, nicely phrased, would have earned his good opinion.'

Lucy said 'Yes, Father,' meekly, privately of the opinion that it wouldn't have made a scrap of difference if she had gone down on her knees to the wretched man. It was her mother who remarked gently: 'Yes, dear, but you must remember that Lucy has always been an honest child; she spoke her mind and I can't blame her. She should never have had to attend his lecture in the first place.'

'Then she wouldn't have seen this magnificent specimen of manhood,' said Jerry, reaching for the cheese.

'Not sweet on him, are you, Sis?' asked Paul slyly, and Lucy being Lucy took his question seriously.

'Oh, no—chalk and cheese, you know. I expect he eats his lunch at Claridges when he's not giving

learned advice to someone or other and making pots
of money with private patients.'

'You're being flippant, my dear.' Her father smiled
at her.

'Yes, Father. I'm sure he's a very clever man and
probably quite nice to the people he likes—anyway,
I shan't see him again, shall I?' She spoke cheerfully,
conscious of a vague regret. She had, after all, only
seen one facet of the man, all the others might be
something quite different.

She spent her nights off doing all the things she
liked doing most; gardening, picking fruit and flowers, driving her father round his sprawling parishes
and tootling round the lanes on small errands for her
mother, and not lonely at all, for although the boys
were away all day, working for a local farmer during
the long vacation, Kitty was home and in the evenings after tea they all gathered in the garden to play
croquet or just sit and talk. The days went too
quickly, and although she returned to the hospital
cheerfully enough it was a sobering thought that
when she next returned in a month's time, it would
be September and autumn.

Once a month wasn't enough, she decided as she
climbed the plain, uncarpeted stairs in the Nurses'
Home, but really she couldn't afford more and her
parents had enough on their plate while the boys
were at university. In less than a year she would
qualify and get a job nearer home and spend all her

days off there. She unpacked her case and went in search of any of her friends who might be around. Angela from Women's Surgical was in the kitchenette making tea; they shared the pot and gossiped comfortably until it was time to change into uniform and go on duty for the night.

The nights passed rapidly. Children's was always full, as fast as one cot was emptied and its small occupant sent triumphantly home, another small creature took its place. Broken bones, hernias, intussusceptions, minor burns, she tended them all with unending patience and a gentleness which turned her small plain face to beauty.

It was two weeks later, when she was on nights off again, that Lucy saw Mr der Linssen. This time she was standing at a zebra crossing in Knightsbridge, having spent her morning with her small nose pressed to the fashionable shop windows there, and among the cars which pulled up was a Panther 4.2 convertible with him in the driving seat. There was a girl beside him; exactly right for the car, too, elegant and dark and haughty. Mr der Linssen, waiting for the tiresome pedestrians to cross the street, allowed his gaze to rest on Lucy, but as no muscle of his face altered, she concluded that he hadn't recognised her. A not unremarkable thing; she was hardly outstanding in the crowd struggling to the opposite pavement—mousy hair and last year's summer dress hardly added up to the spectacular.

But the next time they met was quite another kettle of fish. Lucy had crossed the busy street outside the hospital to purchase fish and chips for such of the night nurses who had been out that morning and now found themselves too famished to go to their beds without something to eat. True, they hadn't been far, only to the Royal College of Surgeons to view its somewhat gruesome exhibits, under Sister Tutor's eagle eye, but they had walked there and back, very neat in their uniforms and caps, and now their appetites had been sharpened, and Lucy, judged to be the most appropriate of them to fetch the food because she was the only one who didn't put her hair into rollers before she went to bed, had nipped smartly across between the buses and cars and vans, purchased mouthwatering pieces of cod in batter and a large parcel of chips, and was on the point of nipping back again when a small boy darted past her and ran into the street, looking neither left nor right as he went.

There were cars and buses coming both ways and a taxi so close that only a miracle would stop it. Lucy plunged after him with no very clear idea as to what she was going to do. She was aware of the taxi right on top of her, the squealing of brakes as the oncoming cars skidded to a halt, then she had plucked the boy from under the taxi's wheels, lurched away and with him and the fish and chips clasped to her bosom, tripped over, caught by the taxi's bumper.

She wasn't knocked out; she could hear the boy yelling from somewhere underneath her and there was a fishy smell from her parcels as they squashed flat under her weight. The next moment she was being helped to her feet.

'Well, well,' observed Mr der Linssen mildly, 'you again.' He added quite unnecessarily: 'You smell of fish.'

She looked at him in a woolly fashion and then at the willing helpers lifting the boy up carefully. He was screaming his head off and Mr der Linssen said: 'Hang on, I'll just take a look.'

It gave her a moment to pull herself together, something which she badly needed to do—a nice burst of tears, which would have done her a lot of good, had to be squashed. She stood up straight, a deplorable figure, smeared with pieces of fish and mangled chips, her uniform filthy and torn and her cap crooked. The Panther, she saw at once, was right beside the taxi, and the same girl was sitting in it. Doctor der Linssen, with the boy in his arms, was speaking to her now. The girl hardly glanced at the boy, only nodded in a rather bored way and then looked at Lucy with a mocking little smile, but that didn't matter, because she was surrounded by people now, patting her on the shoulder, telling her that she was a brave girl and asking if she were hurt; she had no chance to answer any of them because Mr der Linssen, with the boy still bawling in his arms,

marched her into Casualty without further ado, said
in an authoritative way: 'I don't think this boy's hurt,
but he'll need a good going over,' laid him on an
examination couch and turned his attention to Lucy.
'You had a nasty thump from that bumper—where
was it exactly?' and when she didn't answer at once:
'There's no need to be mealy-mouthed about it—
your behind, I take it—better get undressed and get
someone to look at it…'

'I wasn't being mealy-mouthed,' said Lucy pettishly, 'I was trying to decide exactly which spot hurt
most.'

He smiled in what she considered to be an unpleasant manner. 'Undress anyway, and I'll get
someone along to see to it. It was only a glancing
blow, but you're such a scrap of a thing you're probably badly bruised.' To her utter astonishment he
added: 'For whom were the fish and chips? If you'll
let me know I'll see that they get a fresh supply—
you've got most of what you bought smeared over
you.'

She said quite humbly: 'Thank you, that would be
kind. They were for the night nurses on the surgical
wards…eight cod pieces and fifty pence worth of
chips. They're waiting for them before they go to
bed—over in the Home.' She added: 'I'm sorry I
haven't any more money with me—I'll leave it in an
envelope at the Lodge for you, sir.'

He only smiled, pushed her gently into one of the

bays and pulled the curtains and turned to speak to Casualty Sister. Lucy couldn't hear what he was saying and she didn't care. The couch looked very inviting and she was suddenly so sleepy that even her aching back didn't matter. She took off her uniform and her shoes and stretched herself out on its hard leather surface, muffled to the eyes with the cosy red blanket lying at its foot. She was asleep within minutes.

She woke reluctantly to Casualty Sister's voice, begging her to rouse herself. 'Bed for you, Nurse Prendergast,' said that lady cheerfully, 'and someone will have another look at you tomorrow and decide if you're fit for duty then. Bad bruising and a few abrasions, but nothing else. Mr der Linssen examined you with Mr Trevett; you couldn't have had better men.' She added kindly: 'There's a porter waiting with a chair, he'll take you over to the home—Home Sister's waiting to help you into a nice hot bath and give you something to eat—after that you can sleep your head off.'

'Yes, Sister. Why did Mr der Linssen need to examine me?'

Sister was helping her to her reluctant feet. 'Well, dear, he was here—and since he'd been on the spot, as it were, he felt it his duty…by the way, I was to tell you that the food was delivered, whatever that means, and the police have taken eye-witness accounts and they'll come and see you later.' She smiled hugely. 'Little heroine, aren't you?'

'Is the boy all right, Sister?'

'He's in Children's, under observation, but nothing much wrong with him, I gather. And now if you're ready, Nurse.'

Lucy was off for two days and despite the stiffness and bruising, she hadn't enjoyed herself so much for some time. The Principal Nursing Officer paid her a stately visit, praised her for her quick action in saving the boy and added that the hospital was proud of her, and Lucy, sitting gingerly on a sore spot, listened meekly; she much preferred Home Sister's visits, for that lady was a cosy middle-aged woman who had had children of her own and knew about tempting appetites and sending in pots of tea when Lucy's numerous friends called in to see her. Indeed, her room was the focal point of a good deal of noise and laughter and a good deal of joking, too, about Mr der Linssen's unexpected appearance.

He had disappeared again, of course. Lucy was visited by Mr Trevett, but there was no sign of his colleague, nor was he mentioned; and a good thing too, she thought. On neither of the occasions upon which they had met had she exactly shone. She dismissed him from her mind because, as she told herself sensibly, there was no point in doing anything else.

She was forcibly reminded of him later that day

when Home Sister came in with a great sheaf of summer flowers, beautifully ribboned. She handed it to Lucy with a comfortable: 'Well, Nurse, whatever you may think about consultants, here's one who appreciates you.'

She smiled nicely without mockery or envy. It was super, thought Lucy, that the hospital still believed in the old- fashioned Home Sister and hadn't had her displaced by some official, who, not being a nurse, had no personal interest in her charges.

There was a card with the flowers. The message upon it was austere: 'To Miss Prendergast with kind regards, Fraam der Linssen.'

Lucy studied it carefully. It was a kind gesture even if rather on the cold side. And what a very peculiar name!

It was decided that instead of going on night duty the next day, Lucy should have her nights off with the addition of two days' sick leave. She didn't feel in the least sick, but she was still sore, and parts of her person were all colours of the rainbow and Authority having decreed it, who was she to dispute their ruling?

Her family welcomed her warmly, but beyond commending her for conduct which he, good man that he was, took for granted, her father had little to say about her rescue of the little boy. Her brothers teased her affectionately, but it was her mother who said: 'Your father is so proud of you, darling, and so are the boys, but you know what boys are.' They smiled at each other. 'I'm proud of you too—you're such a small creature and you could have been mown down.' Mrs Prendergast smiled again, rather mistily. 'That nice man who stopped and took you both into the hospital wrote me a letter—I've got it here; I thought you might like to see it—a Dutch name, too. I suppose he was just passing...'

'He's the lecturer—you remember, Mother? When I fell asleep.'

Her mother giggled. 'Darling—I didn't know, do tell me all about it.'

Lucy did, and now that it was all over and done with she laughed just as much as her mother over the fish and chips.

'But what a nice man to get you another lot—he sounds a poppet.'

Lucy said that probably he was, although she didn't believe that Mr der Linssen was quite the type one would describe as a poppet. Poppets were plump and cosy and good-natured, and he was none of these. She read his letter, sitting on the kitchen table eating the bits of pastry left over from the pie her mother was making, and had to admit that it was a very nice one, although she didn't believe the bit where he wrote that he admired her for bravery. He hadn't admired her in the least, on the contrary he had complained that she smelt of fish...but the flowers had been lovely even if he'd been doing the polite thing; probably his secretary had bought them. She folded the letter up carefully. 'He sent me some flowers,' she told her mother, 'but I expect he only did it because he thought he should.'

Her mother put the pie in the oven. 'I expect so, too, darling,' she said carefully casual.

Lucy was still sitting there, swinging her rather nice legs, when her father came in to join them. 'Never let it be said,' he observed earnestly, 'that virtue has no reward. You remember my friend Theodul de Groot? I've just received a telephone call from him; he's in London attending some medical seminar or other, and asks particularly after you, Lucy. Indeed he wished to know if you have any holiday due and if so would you like to pay him a visit. Mies liked you when you met seven—eight? years ago and you're of a similar age. I daresay she's lonely now that her mother is dead. Do you have any holiday, my dear?'

'Yes,' said Lucy very fast, 'two weeks due and I'm to take them at the end of next week—that's when I come off night duty.'

'Splendid—he'll be in London for a few days yet, but he's anxious to come and see us. I'm sure he will be willing to stay until you're free and take you back with him.'

'You would like to go, love?' asked her mother.

'Oh, rather—it'll be super! I loved it when I went

before, but that's ages ago—I was at school. Does Doctor de Groot still practise?'

'Oh, yes. He has a large practice in Amsterdam still, mostly poor patients, I believe, but he has a splendid reputation in the city and numbers a great many prominent men among his friends.'

'And Mies? I haven't heard from her for ages.'

'She helps her father—receptionist and so on, I gather. But I'm sure she'll have plenty of free time to spend with you.'

'Wouldn't it be strange if you met that lecturer while you were there?' Mrs Prendergast's tone was artless.

'Well, I shan't. I should think he lived in London, wouldn't you?' Lucy ran her finger round the remains of custard in a dish and licked it carefully. 'I wonder what clothes I should take?'

The rest of her nights off were spent in pleasurable planning and she went back happily enough to finish her night duty, her bruises now an unpleasant yellow. The four nights went quickly enough now that she had something to look forward to, even though they were busier than ever, what with a clutch of very ill babies to be dealt with hourly and watched over with care, and two toddlers who kept the night hours as noisy as the day with their cries of rage because they wanted to go home.

Lucy had just finished the ten o'clock feeds on her last night, and was trying to soothe a very small, very angry baby, when Mr Henderson, the Surgical Registrar, came into the ward, and with him Mr der Linssen. At the sight of them the baby yelled even louder, as red in the face and as peppery as an ill-tempered colonel, so that Lucy, holding him with one hand over her shoulder while she straightened the cot with the other, looked round to see what was putting the infant into an even worse rage.

'Mr der Linssen wants a word with you, Nurse Prendergast,' said the Registrar importantly, and she frowned at him; he was a short, pompous man who always made the babies cry, not because he was unkind to them but because he disliked having them sick up on his coat and sometimes worse than that, and they must have known it. 'Put him back in the cot, Nurse.'

She had no intention of doing anything of the sort, but Mr der Linssen stretched out a long arm and took the infant from her, settling him against one great shoulder, where, to her great annoyance, it stopped bawling at once, hiccoughed loudly and went to sleep, its head tucked against the superfine wool of his jacket. Lucy, annoyed that the baby should put her in a bad light, hoped fervently that it would dribble all over him.

'Babies like me,' observed Mr der Linssen smugly, and then: 'I hear from Mr Trevett that you are going to your home tomorrow. I have to drive to Bristol—I'll give you a lift.'

She eyed him frostily. 'How kind, but I'm going by train.' She added: 'Beaminster's rather out of your way.'

'A part of England I have always wished to see,' he assured her airily. 'Will ten o'clock suit you?' He smiled most engagingly. 'You may sleep the whole way if you wish.'

In other words, she thought ungraciously, he couldn't care less whether I'm there or not, and then went pink as he went on: 'I should much prefer you to stay awake, but never let it be said that I'm an unreasonable man.'

He handed the baby back and it instantly started screaming its head off again. 'Ten o'clock?' he repeated. It wasn't a question, just a statement of fact.

Lucy was already tired and to tell the truth the prospect of a long train journey on top of a busy night wasn't all that enthralling. 'Oh, very well,' she said ungraciously, and had a moment's amusement at the Registrar's face.

Mr der Linssen's handsome features didn't alter. He nodded calmly and went away.

CHAPTER TWO

LUCY SAT stiffly in the comfort of the Panther as Mr
der Linssen cut a swathe through the London traffic
and drove due west. It seemed that he was as good
at driving a car as he was at soothing a baby and just
as patient; through the number of hold-ups they were
caught up in he sat quietly, neither tapping an impatient tattoo with his long, well manicured fingers,
nor muttering under his breath; in fact, beyond wishing her a cheerful good morning when she had presented herself, punctual but inimical, at the hospital
entrance, he hadn't spoken. She was wondering
about that when he observed suddenly: 'Still feeling
cross? No need; I am at times ill-tempered, arrogant
and inconsiderate, but I do not bear malice and nor—
as I suspect you are thinking—am I heaping coals of
fire upon your mousy head because you dropped off
during one of my lectures...It was a good lecture
too.'

And how did she answer that? thought Lucy, and
need he have reminded her that her hair was mousy?
She almost exploded when he added kindly: 'Even
if it is mousy it is always clean and shining. Don't
ever give it one of those rinses—my young sister did

28

and ended up with bright red streaks in all the wrong places.'

'Have you got a sister?' she was surprised into asking.

'Lord, yes, and years younger than I am. You sound surprised.'

He was working his way towards the M3 and she looked out at the river as they crossed Putney Bridge and swept on towards Richmond. She said slowly, not wishing to offend him even though she didn't think she liked him at all: 'Well, I am, a bit… I mean when one gets—gets older one talks about a wife and children…'

'But I have neither, as I have already told you. You mean perhaps that I am middle-aged. Well, I suppose I am; nudging forty is hardly youth.'

'The prime of life,' said Lucy. 'I'm twenty-three, but women get older much quicker than men do.'

He drove gently through the suburbs. 'That I cannot believe, what with hairdressers and beauty parlours and an endless succession of new clothes.'

Probably he had girl-friends who enjoyed these aids to youth and beauty, reflected Lucy; it wasn't much use telling him that student nurses did their own hair, sleeping in rollers which kept them awake half the night in the pursuit of beauty, and as for boutiques and up-to-the-minute clothes, they either made their own or shopped at Marks & Spencer or C. & A.

She said politely: 'I expect you're right' and then made a banal remark about the weather and presently, when they reached the motorway and were doing a steady seventy, she closed her eyes and went to sleep.

She woke up just before midday to find that they were already on the outskirts of Sherborne and to her disjointed apologies he rejoined casually: 'You needed a nap. We'll have coffee—is there anywhere quiet and easy to park?'

She directed him to an old timbered building opposite the Abbey where they drank coffee and ate old-fashioned currant buns, and nicely refreshed with her sleep and the food, Lucy told him about the little town. 'We don't come here often,' she observed. 'Crewkerne is nearer, and anyway we can always go into Beaminster.'

'And that is a country town?' he asked idly.

'Well, it's a large village, I suppose.'

He smiled. 'Then let us go and inspect this village, shall we? Unless you could eat another bun?'

She assured him that she had had enough and feeling quite friendly towards him, she climbed back into the car and as he turned back into the main street to take the road to Crewkerne she apologised again, only to have the little glow of friendliness doused by his casual: 'You are making too much of a brief doze, Lucy. I did tell you that you could sleep all the way if you wished to.' He made it worse by adding:

'I'm only giving you a lift, you know, you don't have to feel bound to entertain me.'

A remark which annoyed her so much that she had to bite her tongue to stop it from uttering the pert retort which instantly came to her mind. She wouldn't speak to him, she decided, and then had to when he asked: 'Just where do I turn off?'

They arrived at the Rectory shortly before two o'clock and she invited him, rather frostily, to meet her family, not for a moment supposing that he would wish to do so, so she was surprised when he said readily enough that he would be delighted.

She led the way up the short drive and opened the door wider; it was already ajar, for her father believed that he should always be available at any time. There was a delicious smell coming from the kitchen and when Lucy called: 'Mother?' her parent called: 'Home already, darling? Come in here—I'm dishing up.'

'Just a minute,' said Lucy to her companion, and left him standing in the hall while she joined her mother. It was astonishing what a lot she could explain in a few seconds; she left Mrs Prendergast in no doubt as to what she was to say to her visitor. 'And tell Father,' whispered Lucy urgently, 'he's not to know that I'm going to Holland.' She added in an artificially high voice: 'Do come and meet Mr der Linssen, Mother, he's been so kind...'

The subject of their conversation was standing

where she had left him, looking amused, but he
greeted Mrs Prendergast charmingly and then made
small talk with Lucy in the sitting room while her
mother went in search of the Rector. That gentleman,
duly primed by his wife, kissed his youngest daughter with affection, looking faintly puzzled and then
turned his attention to his guest. 'A drink?' he suggested hospitably, 'and of course you will stay to
lunch.'

Mr der Linssen shot a sidelong glance at Lucy's
face and his eyes gleamed with amusement at its expression. 'There is nothing I should have liked better,' he said pleasantly, 'but I have an appointment
and dare not stay.' He shot a look under his lids at
Lucy as he spoke and saw relief on her face.

Her mother saw it too: 'Then another time, Mr der
Linssen—we should be so glad to give you lunch
and the other children would love to meet you.'

'You have a large family, Mrs Prendergast?'

She beamed at him. 'Five—Lucy's the youngest.'

The rector chuckled. 'And the plainest, poor
child—she takes after me.'

Lucy went bright pink. Really, her father was a
darling but said all the wrong things sometimes, and
it gave Mr der Linssen the chance to look amused
again. She gave him a glassy stare while he shook
hands with her parents and wished him an austere
goodbye and added thanks cold enough to freeze his
bones. Not that he appeared to notice; his goodbye

to her was casual and friendly, he even wished her a pleasant holiday.

She didn't go to the door to see him off and when her mother came indoors she tried to look nonchalant under that lady's searching look. 'Darling,' said her mother, 'did you have to be quite so terse with the poor man? Such a nice smile too. He must have been famished.'

Lucy's mousy brows drew together in a frown. 'Oh, lord—I didn't think—we did stop in Sherborne for coffee and buns, though.'

'My dear,' observed her mother gently, 'he is a very large man, I hardly feel that coffee and buns would fill him up.' She swept her daughter into the kitchen and began to dish up dinner. 'And why isn't he to know that you're going to Holland?' she enquired mildly.

Lucy, dishing up roast potatoes, felt herself blushing again and scowled. 'Well, if I'd told him, he might have thought…that is, it would have looked as though… Oh, dear, that sounds conceited, but I don't mean it to be, Mother.'

'You don't want to be beholden to him, darling,' suggested her mother helpfully.

Lucy sighed, relieved that her mother understood. 'Yes, that's it.' She took a potato out of the dish and nibbled at it. 'Is it just the three of us?'

'Yes, love—the others will come in this evening, I hope—the boys just for the night to see your god-

father. Kitty's visiting Agnes'—Agnes was a bosom
friend in Yeovil—'but she'll be back for supper and
Emma will come over for an hour while Will minds
the twins.'

'Oh, good—then I'll have time to pack after dinner.'

She hadn't many clothes and those that she had
weren't very exciting; she went through her wardrobe with a dissatisfied frown, casting aside so much
that she was forced to do it all over again otherwise
she would have had nothing to take with her. In the
end she settled for a jersey dress and jacket, a swim-
suit in case it was warm enough to swim, a tweed
skirt she really rather hated because she had had it
for a couple of years now, slacks and a variety of
shirts and sweaters. It was September now and it
could turn chilly and she would look a fool in thin
clothes. She had two evening dresses, neither of them
of the kind to turn a man's head, even for a moment.
It was a pity that both her sisters were tall shapely
girls. She rummaged round some more and came
upon a cotton skirt, very full and rose-patterned; it
might do for an evening, if they were to go out, and
there was a silk blouse somewhere—she had almost
thrown it away because she was so heartily sick of
it, but it would do at a pinch, she supposed. She
packed without much pleasure and when her mother
put her head round the door to see how she was
getting on, assured her that she had plenty of clothes;

she was only going for a fortnight, anyway. She added her raincoat and a handful of headscarves and went to look at her shoes. Not much there, she reflected; her good black patent and the matching handbag, some worthy walking shoes which she might need and some rather fetching strapped shoes which would do very well for the evenings. She added a dressing gown, undies and slippers to the pile on the bed and then, because she could hear a car driving up to the Rectory, decided to pack them later with her other things; that would be her father's friend, Doctor de Groot.

She had forgotten how nice he was; elderly and stooping a little with twinkling blue eyes and a marked accent. Her holiday was going to be fun after all; she sat in the midst of her family and beamed at everyone.

They set off the next morning, and it didn't take Lucy long to discover that the journey wasn't going to be a dull one. Doctor de Groot, once in the driver's seat of his Mercedes, turned from a mild, elderly man with a rather pedantic manner into a speed fiend, who swore—luckily in his own language—at every little hold-up, every traffic light against him and any car which dared to overtake him. By the time they reached Dover, she had reason to be glad that she was by nature a calm girl, otherwise she might have been having hysterics. They had to wait in the queue for the Hovercraft too, a circumstance which caused her companion to drum on the wheel, mutter a good deal and generally fidget around, so that it was a relief when they went on board. Once there and out of his car, he reverted to the mild elderly gentleman again, which was a mercy, for they hadn't stopped on the journey and his solicitous attention was very welcome. Lucy retired to the ladies' and did her hair and her face, then returned to her seat to find that he had ordered coffee and sandwiches. It took quite a lot of self-control not to wolf them and then help herself to his as well.

They seemed to be in Calais in no time at all and Lucy, fortified with the sandwiches, strapped herself into her seat and hoped for the best. Not a very good best, actually, for Doctor de Groot was, if anything, slightly more maniacal on his own side of the Channel, and now, of course, they were driving on the other side of the road. They were to go along the coast, he explained, and cross over into Holland at the border town of Sluis, a journey of almost two hundred and thirty miles all told. 'We shall be home for supper,' he told her. 'We don't need to stop for tea, do we?'

It seemed a long way, but at the speed they were going she reflected that it wouldn't take all that long. Doctor de Groot blandly ignored the speed signs and tore along the straight roads at a steady eighty miles an hour, only slowing for towns and villages. He had had to go more slowly in France and Belgium, of course, for there weren't many empty stretches of road, but once in Holland, on the motorway, he put his foot down and kept it there.

It seemed no time at all before they were in the outskirts of Amsterdam, but all the same Lucy was glad to see the staid blocks of flats on either side of them. She was tired and hungry and at the back of her mind was a longing to be at home in her mother's kitchen, getting the supper. But she forgot that almost as soon as she had thought it; the flats might look rather dull from the outside, but their lighted windows with the curtains undrawn gave glimpses of cosy interiors. She wondered what it would be like to live like that, boxed up in a big city with no fields at the back door, no garden even. Hateful, and yet in the older part of the city there were lovely steepled houses, old and narrow with important front doors which opened on to hidden splendours which the passer-by never saw. To live in one of those, she conceded, would be a delight.

She caught glimpses of them now as they neared the heart of the city and crossed the circular *grachten* encircling it, each one looking like a Dutch old master. She craned her neck to see them better but remembered to recognise the turning her companion must take to his own home, which delighted him. 'So you remember a little of our city, Lucy?' he asked, well pleased. 'It is beautiful, is it not? You shall explore...'

'Oh, lovely,' declared Lucy, and really meant it. The hair-raising trip from Calais, worse if possible than the drive to Dover from her home, was worth every heart-stopping moment. She could forget it, anyway; she would be going back by boat at the end of her visit and probably Doctor de Groot would be too busy to drive her around. Perhaps Mies had a car…

They were nearing the end of their journey now, the Churchilllaan where Doctor de Groot had a flat, and as it came into view she could see that it hadn't changed at all. It was on the ground floor, surrounded by green lawns and an ornamental canal with ducks on it and flowering shrubs, but no garden of its own. The doctor drew up untidily before the entrance, helped her out and pressed the button which would allow the occupants of the flat to open the front door. 'I have a key,' he explained, 'but Mies likes to know when I am home.'

The entrance was rather impressive, with panelled walls and rather peculiar murals, a staircase wound itself up the side of one wall and there were two lifts facing the door, but the doctor's front door was one of two leading from the foyer and Mies, warned of their coming, was already there.

Mies, unlike her surroundings, had changed quite a lot. Lucy hadn't see her for almost eight years and now, a year younger than she, at twenty-two Mies was quite something—ash-blonde hair, cut short and curling, big blue eyes and a stunning figure. Lucy, not an envious girl by nature, flung herself at her friend with a yelp of delight. 'You're gorgeous!' she declared. 'Who'd have thought it eight years ago—you're a raving beauty, Mies!'

Mies looked pleased. 'You think, yes?' She returned Lucy's hug and then stood back to study her.

'No need,' observed Lucy a little wryly. 'I've not changed, you see.'

Mies made a little face. 'Perhaps not, but your figure is O.K. and your eyes are *extraordinaire*.'

'Green,' said Lucy flatly as she followed the doctor and Mies into the flat.

'You have the same room,' said Mies, 'so that you feel you are at home.' She smiled warmly as she led the way across the wide hall and down a short passage. The flat was a large one, its rooms lofty and well furnished. As far as Lucy could remember, it hadn't changed in the least. She unpacked in her pretty little bedroom and went along to the dining room for supper, a meal they ate without haste, catching up on news and reminding each other of all the things they had done when she had stayed there before.

'I work,' explained Mies, 'for Papa, but now I take a holiday and we go out, Lucy. I have not a car...' she shot a vexed look at her father as she spoke, 'but there are bicycles. You can still use a *fiets*?'

'Oh, rather, though I daresay I'll be scared to death in Amsterdam.'

The doctor glanced up. 'I think that maybe I will take a few hours off and we will take you for a little trip, Lucy. Into the country, perhaps?'

'Sounds smashing,' agreed Lucy happily, 'but just pottering suits me, you know.'

'We will also potter,' declared Mies seriously, 'and you will speak English to me, Lucy, for I am now with rust.' She shrugged her shoulders. 'I speak only a very little and I forget.'

'You'll remember every word in a couple of days,' observed Lucy comfortably. 'I wish I could speak Dutch even half as well.'

Mies poured their after supper coffee. 'Truly? Then we will also speak Dutch and you will learn quickly.'

They spent the rest of the evening telling each other what they did and whether they liked it or not while the doctor retired to his study to read his post. 'I shall marry,' declared Mies, 'it is nice to work for Papa but not for too long, I think. I have many friends but no one that I wish to marry.' She paused. 'At least I think so.'

Lucy thought how nice it must be; so pretty that one could pick and choose instead of just waiting and hoping that one day some man would come along and want to marry one. True, she was only twenty-three, but the years went fast and there were

any number of pretty girls growing up all the time.
Probably she would have to settle for someone who
had been crossed in love and wanted to make a second choice, or a widower with troublesome children,
looking for a sensible woman to mind them; probably
no one would ask her at all. A sudden and quite
surprising memory flashed through her head of Mr
der Linssen and with it a kind of nameless wish that
he could have fallen for her—even for a day or two,
she conceded; it would have done her ego no end of
good.

'You dream?' enquired Mies.

Lucy shook her head. 'What sort of a man are you
going to marry?' she asked.

The subject kept them happily talking until bedtime.

Lucy spent the next two days renewing her acquaintance with Amsterdam; the actual city hadn't
changed, she discovered, only the Kalverstraat was
full of modern shops now, crowding out the small,
expensive ones she remembered, but de Bijenkorf
was still there and so was Vroom and Dreesman, and
C. & A. The pair of them wandered happily from
shop to shop, buying nothing at all and drinking coffee in one of the small coffee bars which were all
over the place. They spent a long time in Krause en
Vogelzang too, looking at wildly expensive undies
and clothes which Mies had made up her mind she
would have if she got married. 'Papa gives me a

salary,' she explained, 'but it isn't much,' she mentioned a sum which was almost twice Lucy's salary—'but when I decide to marry then he will give me all the money I want. I shall have beautiful clothes and the finest linen for my house.' She smiled brilliantly at Lucy. 'And you, your papa will do that for you also?'

'Oh, rather,' agreed Lucy promptly, telling herself that it wasn't really a fib; he would if he had the money. Mies was an only child and it was a little hard for her to understand that not everyone lived in the comfort she had had all her life.

'You shall come to the wedding,' said Mies, tucking an arm into Lucy's, 'and there you will meet a very suitable husband.' She gave the arm a tug. 'Let us drink more coffee before we return home.'

It was during dinner that Doctor de Groot suggested that Lucy might like to see the clinic he had set up in a street off the Haarlemmerdijk. 'Not my own, of course,' he explained, 'but I have the widest support from the Health Service and work closely with the hospital authorities.'

'Every day?' asked Lucy.

'On four days a week, afternoon and evenings. I have my own surgery each morning—you remember it, close by?'

'That's where I work,' interrupted Mies. 'Papa doesn't like me to go to the clinic, only to visit. I shall come with you tomorrow. Shall we go with you, Papa, or take a taxi?'

'Supposing you come in the afternoon? I shall be home for lunch and I can drive you both there, then you can take a taxi home when you are ready.'

The weather had changed in the morning, the bright autumn sunshine had been nudged away by a nippy little wind and billowing clouds. The two girls spent the morning going through Mies' wardrobe while the daily maid did the housework and made the beds and presently brought them coffee.

She prepared most of their lunch too; Lucy, used to giving a hand round the house, felt guilty at doing nothing at all, but Mies, when consulted, had looked quite surprised. 'But of course you do nothing,' she exclaimed, 'Anneke is paid for her work and would not like to be helped, but if you wish we will arrange the table.'

The doctor was a little late for lunch so that they had to hurry over it rather. Lucy, getting into her raincoat and changing her light shoes for her sensible ones, paused only long enough to dab powder on her unpretentious nose, snatch up her shoulder bag, and run back into the hall where he was waiting. They had to wait for Mies, who wasn't the hurrying sort so that he became a little impatient and Lucy hoped that he wouldn't try and make up time driving through the city, but perhaps he was careful in Amsterdam.

He wasn't; he drove like a demented Jehu, spilling out Dutch oaths through clenched teeth and taking hair's-breadth risks between trams and buses, but as Mies sat without turning a hair, Lucy concluded that she must do the same. She had never been so pleased to see anything as their destination when he finally scraped to a halt in a narrow street, lined with grey warehouses and old-fashioned blocks of flats. The clinic was old-fashioned enough too on the outside, but once through its door and down the long narrow passage it was transformed into something very modern indeed; a waiting room on the left; a brightly painted apartment with plenty of chairs, coffee machine, papers and magazines on several well-placed tables and a cheerful elderly woman sitting behind a desk in one corner, introduced by the doctor as Mevrouw Valker. And back in the passage again, the end door revealed another wide passage with several doors leading from it; consulting rooms, treatment rooms, an X-ray department, cloakrooms and a small changing room for the staff.

'Very nice,' declared Lucy, poking her inquisitive nose round every door. 'Do you specialise or is it general?'

'I suppose one might say general, although we deal largely with Reynaud's disease and thromboangiitis obliterans—inflammation of the blood vessels—a distressing condition, probably you have never encountered it, Lucy.'

She said, quite truthfully that no, she hadn't, and forbore to mention that she had slept through a masterly lecture upon it, and because she still found the memory of it disquieting, changed the subject quickly. The first patients began to arrive presently and she and Mies retired to an empty consulting room, so that Mies could explain exactly how the clinic was run. 'Of course, Papa receives an honorarium, but it is not very much, you understand, and there are many doctors who come here also to give advice and help him too and they receive nothing at all, for they do not wish it—the experience is great.' She added in a burst of honesty: 'Papa is very clever, but not as clever as some of the doctors and surgeons who come here to see the patients.'

'Do they pay?' Lucy wanted to know.

'There are those who do; those who cannot are treated free. It—how do you say?—evens up.'

Lucy was peering in the well equipped cupboards. 'You don't work here?'

'No—it is not a very nice part of the city and Papa does not like me to walk here alone. When we wish to go we shall telephone for a taxi.'

Lucy, who had traipsed some pretty grotty streets round St Norbert's, suggested that as there would be two of them they would be safe enough, but Mies wasn't going to agree, she could see that, so she contented herself with asking if there was any more to see.

'I think that you have seen all,' said Mies, and turned round as her father put his head round the door. 'Tell Mevrouw Valker to keep the boy van Berends back—she can send the patient after him.' He spoke in English, for he was far too polite to speak Dutch in front of Lucy, and Mies said at once: 'Certainly, Papa. I'll go now.'

The two girls went into the passage together and Mies disappeared into the waiting room, leaving Lucy to dawdle towards the entrance for lack of anything better to do. She was almost at the door when it opened.

'Well, well, the parson's daughter!' exclaimed Mr der Linssen as he shut it behind him.

'Well, you've no reason to make it sound as though I were exhibit A at an old-tyme exhibition,' snapped Lucy, her temper fired by the faint mockery with which he was regarding her.

He gave a shout of laughter. 'And you haven't lost that tongue of yours either,' he commented. 'Always ready with an answer, aren't you?'

He took off his car coat and hung it any old how on a peg on the wall. 'How did you get here?'

Very much on her dignity she told him. 'And how did you get here?' she asked in a chilly little voice.

He frowned her down. 'I hardly think…' he began, and then broke off to exclaim: 'Mies—more beautiful than ever! Why haven't I seen you lately?'

Mies had come out of the waiting room and now,

with every appearance of delight, had skipped down the passage to fling herself at him. 'Fraam, how nice to see you! You are always so busy...and here is my good friend Lucy Prendergast.'

He bent and kissed her lovely face. 'Yes, we've met in England.' He turned round and kissed Lucy too in an absent-minded manner. 'I've just one check to make. Wait and I'll give you a lift back.'

He had gone while Lucy was still getting her breath back.

Mies took her arm and led her back to the room they had been in. 'Now that is splendid, that you know Fraam. Is he not handsome? And he is also rich and not yet married, even though he has all the girls to choose from.' She giggled. 'I think that I shall marry him; I am a little in love with him, you know, although he is old, and he is devoted to me. Would we not make a nice pair?'

Lucy eyed her friend. 'Yes, as a matter of fact, you would, and you're a doctor's daughter, too, you know what to expect if you marry him.'

'That is true, but you must understand that he is not a house doctor, he is consultant surgeon with many hospitals and travels to other countries. He has a practice of course in the best part of Amsterdam, but he works in many of the clinics also. He has a large house, too.'

'It sounds just right,' observed Lucy. 'You wouldn't want to marry a poor man, would you?'

Mies looked horrified. 'Oh, no, I could not. And you, Lucy? You would also wish to marry a man with money?'

She was saved from answering by the entrance of a young man. He was tall and thin and studious-looking, with fair hair, steady blue eyes and a ready smile. He spoke to Mies in Dutch and she answered him in what Lucy considered to be a very off-hand way before switching to English.

'This is Willem de Vries, Lucy—he is a doctor also and works at the Grotehof Ziekenhuis. He comes here to work with Papa.' She added carelessly: 'I have known him for ever.'

Willem looked shy and Lucy made haste to say how glad she was to meet him and added a few rather inane remarks because the atmosphere seemed a little strained. 'Did you go to school together?' she asked chattily, and just as he was on the point of replying, Mies said quickly: 'Yes, we did. Willem, should you not be working?'

He nodded and then asked hesitantly: 'We'll see each other soon?' and had to be content with her brief, 'I expect so. You can take us to a *bioscoop* one evening if you want to.'

After he had gone there was a short silence while Lucy tried to think of something casual to say, but it was Mies who spoke first. 'Willem is a dull person. I have known him all my life, and besides, he does not kiss and laugh like Fraam.'

'I thought he looked rather a dear. How old is he?'

'Twenty-six. Fraam is going to be forty soon.'

'Poor old Fraam,' said Lucy naughtily, and then caught her breath when he said from the door behind her:

'Your concern for my advanced age does you credit, Miss Prendergast.'

She turned round and looked at him; of course she would be Miss Prendergast from now on because she had had the nerve to call him Fraam, a liberty he would repay four-fold, she had no doubt. She said with an airiness she didn't quite feel: 'Hullo. Listeners never hear any good of themselves,' and added: 'Mr der Linssen.'

His smile was frosty. 'But you are quite right, Miss Prendergast. It is a pity that we do not all have the gift of dropping off when we do not wish to listen, though.'

Her green eyes sparked temper. 'What a very unfair thing to say—you know quite well that I'd been up all night!'

Mies was staring at them both in turn. 'Don't you like each other?' she asked in an interested way.

'That remains to be seen,' observed Mr der Linssen, and he smiled in what Lucy considered to be a nasty fashion. 'Our acquaintance is so far of the very slightest.'

'Oh, well,' declared Mies a little pettishly, 'you will have to become friends, for it is most disagreeable when two people meet and do not speak.' Her tone changed to charming beguilement. 'Fraam, do you go to the hospital dance next Saturday? Would you not like to take me?' She added quickly: 'Willem can take Lucy.'

Lucy, watching his handsome, bland features, waited for him to say 'Poor Willem,' but he didn't, only laughed and said: 'Of course I would like to take you, *schat*, but I have already promised to take Eloise. Besides, surely Willem had already asked you?'

Mies hunched a shoulder. 'Oh, him. Of course he has asked me, but he cannot always have what he wants. And now I must find someone for Lucy.'

They both looked at her thoughtfully, just as though, she fumed silently, I had a wart on my nose or cross-eyes. Out loud she said in a cool voice: 'Oh, is there to be a dance? Well, don't bother about me, Mies, I don't particularly want to go—I'm not all that keen on dancing.'

And that was a wicked lie, if ever there was one; she loved it, what was more, she was very good at it too; once on the dance floor she became a graceful creature, never putting a foot wrong, her almost plain face pink and animated, her green eyes flashing with pleasure. She need not have spoken. Mies said firmly: 'But of course you will come, it is the greatest pleasure, and if you cannot dance then there are always people who do not wish to do so. Professors...'

Mr der Linssen allowed a small sound to escape his lips. 'There are some most interesting professors,' he agreed gravely, 'and now if you two are ready, shall I drive you back?'

'Which car have you?' demanded Mies.

'The Panther.'

She nodded in a satisfied manner. 'Fraam has three cars,' she explained to Lucy, 'the Panther, and a Rolls-Royce Camargue, which I prefer, and also a silly little car, a Mini, handy for town but not very comfortable. Oh, and I forget that he has a Range Rover somewhere in England.'

'I have a bicycle too,' supplied Mr der Linssen, 'and I use it sometimes.' He glanced at Lucy, goggling at such a superfluity of cars. 'It helps to keep old age at bay,' he told her as he opened the door.

Lucy sat in the back as he drove them home, listening to Mies chattering away, no longer needing to speak English, and from the amused chuckles uttered by her companion, they were enjoying themselves. Let them, brooded Lucy, and when they reached the flat, she thanked him in a severe voice for the lift and stood silently while Mies giggled and chattered for another five minutes. Presently, though, he said in English: 'I must go—I have work to do. No, I will not come in for a drink. What would Eloise say if she knew that I was spending so much time with you?' He kissed her on her cheek and looked across at Lucy who had taken a step backwards. She wished she hadn't when she saw the mocking amusement on his face. 'Good night, Miss Prendergast.'

She mumbled in reply and then had to explain to Mies why he kept calling her Miss Prendergast. 'You see, I'm only a student nurse and he's a consultant and so it's not quite the thing to call him Fraam, and now he's put out because I did and that's his way of letting me know that I've been too—too familiar.'

Mies shrieked with laughter. 'Lucy, you are so sweet and so *oudewetse*—old-fashioned, you say?' She tucked an arm under Lucy's. 'Let us have coffee and discuss the dance.'

'I really meant it—that I'd rather not go. Anyway, I don't think I've anything to wear.'

Mies didn't believe her and together they inspected the two dresses Lucy had brought with her. 'They are most *deftig*,' said Mies politely. 'You shall wear this one.' She spread out the green jersey dress Lucy had held up for her inspection. It was very plain, but the colour went well with her eyes and its cut was so simple that it hardly mattered that it was two years old. 'And if you do not dance,' went on Mies, unconsciously cruel, 'no one will notice what you're wearing. I will be sure and introduce you to a great many people who will like to talk to you.'

It sounded as though it was going to be an awful evening, but there would be no difficulty in avoiding Mr der Linssen; there would be a great crush of people, and besides, he would be wholly taken up with his Eloise.

Lucy, in bed, allowed her thoughts to dwell on the enchanting prospect of turning beautiful overnight, and clad in something quite stunning in silk chiffon, taking the entire company at the dance by storm. She would take the hateful Fraam by storm too and when he wanted to dance with her she would turn her back, or perhaps an icy stare would be better?

She slid from her ridiculous daydreaming into sleep.

CHAPTER THREE

LUCY DRESSED very carefully for the dance, and the result, she considered, when she surveyed herself in the looking glass, wasn't too bad. Her mousy hair she had brushed until it shone and then piled in a topknot of sausage curls on the top of her head. It had taken a long time to do, but she was clever at dressing hair although she could seldom be bothered to do it. Her face she had done the best she could with and excitement had given her a pretty colour, so that her eyes seemed more brilliant than ever. And as for the dress, it would do. The colour was pretty and the silk jersey fell in graceful folds, but it was one of thousands like it, and another woman would take it for what it was, something off the peg from a large store; all the same, it would pass in a crowd. She fastened the old-fashioned silver locket on its heavy chain and clasped the thick silver bracelet her father had given her when she was twenty-one, caught up the silver kid purse which matched her sandals and went along to Mies' room to fetch the cloak she was to borrow.

Mies looked like the front cover of *Vogue*; her dress, blue and pleated finely, certainly had never

seen anything as ordinary as a peg; it swirled around
her, its neckline daringly low, its full skirt sweeping
the floor. She whirled round for Lucy to see and
asked: 'I look good, yes?' She was so pleased with
her own appearance that she had time only to com-
ment: 'You look nice, Lucy,' before plunging into
the important matter of deciding which shoes she
should wear. Lucy, arranging Mies' brown velvet
cape round her shoulders, fought a rising envy, feeling ashamed of it; if it wasn't for Mies and her father
she wouldn't be going to a big dance where, she
assured herself, she had every intention of enjoying
herself.

They were a little late getting there and the entrance hall of the hospital was full of people on their
way to leave their wraps, stopping to greet friends as
they went. Doctor de Groot took them both by the
arm and made his way through the crowd and said
with the air of a man determined to do his duty that
he would stay just where he was while they got rid
of their cloaks and when they rejoined him, he offered them each an arm and told them gallantly, if
not truthfully in Lucy's case, that they were the two
prettiest girls there.

The dance was being held in the lecture hall and
a rather noisy band was already on the decorated
platform while the hall itself, transformed for the occasion by quantities of flowers and streamers, was
comfortably filled with dancers. Mies was pounced

upon by Willem the moment they entered, leaving Doctor de Groot to dance with Lucy. He was a poor dancer and she spent most of her time avoiding his feet, and as he was waltzing to a rather spirited rumba, she was hard put to it to fit her steps to his; it hardly augured a jolly evening, she reflected, and then reminded herself that at least she was on the floor and not trying to look unconcerned propped up against a wall.

The band blared itself to a halt and she found herself standing beside Doctor de Groot, and staring at Mr der Linssen who still had an arm round a willowy girl with improbable golden hair worn in a fashionable frizz and wearing a gown with a plunging neckline which Lucy privately considered quite unsuitable to her bony chest. The sight of it made her feel dowdy; her own dress was cut, she had been quick to see, with a much too modest neckline. If she had had a pair of scissors handy, she felt reckless enough to slice the front of it to match the other dresses around her; at least she wasn't bony even if she was small and slim.

She exchanged polite good evenings and was relieved when Mies joined them with the devoted Willem in tow, to kiss Mr der Linssen and shriek something at his companion who shrieked back. She then turned to Lucy to exclaim: 'Is it not the greatest fun? You have danced with Papa? Now I will find you someone to talk to,' she included everyone: 'Lucy does not wish to dance…'

It was Willem who ignored that; as the band struck up once more he smiled at her: 'But with me, once, please?'

It was one of the latest pop tunes; Lucy gave a little nod and followed Willem on to the almost empty floor; perhaps she wouldn't have any more partners for the rest of the evening, but at least she was going to enjoy this. She dipped and twirled and pivoted in her silver sandals, oblivious of the astonished stares from the little group she had just left. It was Mies who said in an amazed voice: 'But she said that she didn't like to dance!'

'She is a mouse of a girl and dowdy,' observed the tall girl, 'but one must say that she can dance.'

Mr der Linssen turned to look at her. 'Is she dowdy?' he asked in an interested voice. 'She seems to me to be quite nicely dressed.'

The two girls looked at him pityingly. 'Fraam, can you not see that it is a dress of two years ago at least which she wears?'

'I can't say that I do.' He sounded bored. 'Shall we join in?'

Lucy had no lack of partners after that. Willem, for all his shyness, had a great many friends; she waltzed and foxtrotted and quickstepped and went to supper with Willem and a party of young men and girls, and if their table was a good deal noisier than any of the others the looks they got were mostly of frank envy, for they were enjoying themselves with a wholeheartedness which was completely unself-conscious.

And after supper, as she was repairing the curly topknot and powdering her nose with Mies, that young lady remarked: 'You dance so well, Lucy, I am surprised, but I am also glad that you enjoy yourself,' she added with unconscious wisdom: 'You see, it has nothing to do with your dress.'

Lucy beamed at her. 'Oh, my dear, if I were wearing a dress like yours I'd be well away—just as you are.'

'But I am not away, I am here.'

'Ah, yes—well, it's a way of saying you're a thundering success.'

'Thundering?'

'Enormous,' explained Lucy patiently. 'Doesn't Willem dance well?'

Mies shrugged. 'Perhaps—I have danced with him so often that I no longer notice.' Her eyes brightened. 'But Fraam—now, he can dance too.'

'Who's the beanpole he's with…the thin girl?'

'That is his current girl-friend. He has many friends but never a close one—that is, girls, you understand.'

They started down the corridor which would take them back to the dance. 'Well, he seems pretty close with you, love,' declared Lucy comfortably.

'I worked on it,' confided her friend, 'but you see I have known him for a long time, just like Willem, and he doesn't—doesn't see me, if you know what I mean.'

'I know just what you mean,' said Lucy.

But apparently Mr der Linssen had seen her, for a little later he cut a polite swathe through the group of young people with whom Lucy was standing, said, equally politely: 'Our dance, I believe, Lucy,' and swung her on to the floor before she could utter whatever she might have uttered if she had had the chance.

After a few surprised moments she said to the pearl stud in his shirt front: 'I suppose you're dancing with me because it's the polite thing to do.'

'I seldom do the polite thing, Miss Prendergast. I wanted to dance with you—you are by far the best dancer here, you know, and I shall be sadly out of fashion if I can't say that I have danced at least once with you.'

For some reason she felt like bursting into tears. After a moment she said in a tight little voice: 'Well, now you have, and I'd like to stop dancing with you, if you don't mind. You're—you're mocking me and in a minute you will have spoilt my evening.'

They were passing one of the doors leading to a corridor outside and he had danced her through it before she could say anything more. 'I'm not mocking you,' he said quietly, 'and if it sounded like it, then I'm sorry. Perhaps we don't always see quite eye to eye, Lucy, but you're not the kind of girl to be mocked, by me or anyone. I'll tell you something else since we're—er—letting our hair down. You look very nice. Oh, I know that your dress isn't the newest fashion, but it's a good deal more becoming than some that are here tonight.' He added: 'I am so afraid that something will slip,' so that she laughed without meaning to. And: 'That's better,' he observed. 'Shall we finish our dance?'

Which they did and as he danced just as well as she did, Lucy enjoyed every minute of it, but at the end he took her back to Doctor de Groot and she didn't speak to him again. She saw him continuously, dancing most of the time with the tall beauty and several times with Mies, but he didn't look at her even, and when eventually the affair finished and they came face to face in the entrance, his good night was said without a smile and carelessly as though she had been a chance partner whom he had managed to remember.

On Monday Doctor de Groot's receptionist, whom Mies helped for the greater part of each day, was ill so that Mies had to go to work, which left Lucy on her own. Not that she minded; she had presents to buy before she went home at the end of the week, and besides, she wanted to roam through the city, taking her own time and going where she fancied.

It was raining on Monday, so she did her shopping, going up Kalverstraat and Leidsestraat doing more looking than buying and enjoying every moment of it. She had a snack lunch at one of the cafés she and Mies had already visited and then, quite uncaring of the heavy rain, wandered off down Nieuwe Spiegelstraat to gaze into the antique dealers' windows there. She got back very wet but entirely satisfied with her day and since Mies would have to work for at least one more day, she planned another outing as she got ready for bed that night.

This time she ignored the shops and main streets and went off down any small street which took her eye, and there were many of them; most of them bisected by a narrow canal bordered by trees and a narrow cobbled road, the lovely houses reflected in the water. She became quite lost presently, but since she had the whole day before her, that didn't worry her, the sun was shining and the sky was a lovely clear blue even though the wind had a chilly nip in it.

It was while she was leaning over a small arched bridge, admiring the patrician houses on either side of the water, that somebody came to a halt beside her. Willem, smiling his nice smile and wishing her a polite good day.

'Well,' said Lucy, 'fancy seeing you here—not that I'm not glad to see you—I'm hopelessly lost.'

'Lost?' he sounded surprised. 'But I thought...' he hesitated and then went on shyly: 'I thought you might be visiting Mr der Linssen, he lives in that large double-fronted house in the centre there.'

He nodded towards a dignified town house with an important front door, wide windows, and a wrought iron railing guarding the double steps leading up to its imposing entrance.

Lucy looked her fill. 'My, my—it looks just like him, too.'

Willem gave her a reproachful look. 'It is a magnificent house.'

'And I'm sure he's a magnificent man and a splendid surgeon,' said Lucy hastily. 'I just meant it looked grand and—well, aloof, if you see what I mean.'

Willem saw, all the same he embarked on a short eulogy about Mr der Linssen. Obviously he was an admirer, fired by a strong urge to follow in his footsteps. Lucy listened with half an ear while she studied the house and wondered what it was like inside. Austere? Dark panelling and red leather? Swedish modern? She would never know. She sighed and Willem said instantly: 'I am free until three o'clock. Would you perhaps have a small lunch with me?'

'Oh, nice—I was just wondering where I should go next. Are we a long way away from the main streets?'

He shook his head. 'No, not if we take short cuts.' He waited patiently while she took another long, lingering look—too lingering, for before she turned away the front door opened and Mr der Linssen came out of his house. He looked, she had to admit, very handsome and very stylish; his tailor's bill must be enormous. She turned away, but not quickly enough; he had seen them, although beyond giving them a hard stare he gave no sign of doing so. Probably he thought she was snooping, just to see where he lived. She went a little pink and marched away so quickly that Willem, for all his long legs, had to hurry to keep up with her.

'You're going the wrong way,' he told her mildly. 'We could have stayed and spoken to Mr der Linssen.'

'Why? He didn't look as though he wanted to know us,' and when she saw the shocked look on his face: 'I'm sorry, but that's what I think—he…at least, I think he doesn't like me.'

Willem gave her a puzzled look. 'Why not? He's nice to everyone, unless he has good reason to be otherwise.'

'Oh, well, we can't all like each other, can we?' She smiled at him. 'Let's have that lunch, shall we?'

They ate toasted sandwiches and drank coffee in a little coffee shop just off the Kalverstraat and presently the talk turned to Mies. It was Willem who brought her into the conversation and Lucy followed his lead because it was quite obvious to her that he wanted to talk about her.

'She's so pretty,' said Willem, 'but she's known

me for years and I'm just a friend.' He looked stricken. 'She doesn't even see me sometimes.'

'Just because you are a friend,' explained Lucy. 'Now if something were to happen—if you fell for another girl perhaps, or lost your temper with Mies— I mean really lose it, Willem, or weren't available when she wanted you, then she would look at you.'

He looked surprised. 'Oh, would she? But I haven't got a bad temper; I just can't feel angry with her, and if she asked me to do something for her I'd never be able to refuse…'

'Then you're going to fall for a girl,' said Lucy. 'How about me?'

Willem's mild eyes popped. 'But I haven't…'

'Don't be silly, of course you haven't, but can't you pretend just a bit? Just enough to make her notice?'

'Well, do you think it would work? And wouldn't you mind?'

'Lord, no,' she spoke cheerfully, aware of an unhappy feeling somewhere deep inside her. 'It might work—only I'm only here for five more days, you know. You'll have to start right away.' She paused to think. 'I'll just mention that I've spent the afternoon with you and this evening you can ring me up…'

'What about?'

'Oh, anything, just so long as you do it—recite a

poem or something. Then I'll say that you're taking me out tomorrow.'

'But I can't—I'm on duty.'

She sighed. 'Willem, you have to—to play-act a bit, never mind if you're on duty—so what? Mies won't know, will she? If you're off in the evening you can come round and take me out for a drink; ask her too and then pay attention to me, if you see what I mean.'

Willem was a dear but not very quick-witted. 'Yes, but then Mies will think…'

'Just what you want her to think—treat her like an old, old friend.'

'She is an old…' He caught Lucy's exasperated eye. 'Oh, well, yes, I see what you mean. All right.'

They parted presently, Willem to his duty in the hospital, Lucy to return to the flat, brooding over what she would say and hoping that it would work. And she supposed that she would have to apologise to Mr der Linssen when she had the chance.

That chance came long before she expected it. The flat was empty when she got to it, Mies was still at the surgery with her father and the housekeeper was out shopping so that when the door bell rang Lucy, armed with the list of likely callers which Mies had thoughtfully drawn up for her, went to answer it. It could be clothes back from the cleaners, the man to see to the fridge, the piano tuner… She opened the door, confident that she was quite able to deal with all or any one of them. Only it wasn't anyone on her list; it was Mr der Linssen standing there, looking rather nice until he saw who she was and his face iced over. She wished that his blue eyes weren't so hard as she wished him a rather faint good afternoon and added in a small voice: 'I'm afraid there's no one else here but me.'

He looked over her shoulder at nothing in particular. 'In that case perhaps I may come in and leave a note for Doctor de Groot.' He spoke so politely that she almost smiled at him and then turned it off just in time as he observed: 'Don't let me keep you from whatever you are doing.'

'I'm not doing anything—I've only just got back…' It seemed the right moment to explain the afternoon's little episode. 'You must have thought me very rude this afternoon, staring at your house like that, only I didn't know it was yours. I'd got lost and then Willem came along and explained where I was and told me where you lived. I could see that you were annoyed.'

'Indeed?' He had paused in his writing of the note to look at her and his eyebrows asked such an obvious question that she felt bound to go on.

'Well, yes—you didn't take any notice of us at all, did you? It was just as though you didn't see me.'

'Your powers of observation are excellent, Miss Prendergast. You were quite right, I do my utmost not to see you, although since we seem to bump into each other far too frequently, I find it becomes increasingly difficult.' He handed her the note. 'Perhaps you will give this to Doctor de Groot when he returns.'

She took it in a nerveless hand and said something she hadn't meant to say at all. 'Are you going to marry that girl—the beautiful one you danced with?'

He looked so thunderous that she took a step backwards. 'If I do, it will be entirely your fault,' he flung at her, and made for the door.

Anyone else would have left it prudently there, but not Lucy. She asked: 'Why do you say that? If you dislike me as much as all that I can't see that it makes any difference whom you marry.' She added kindly: 'There's no need to get so worked up about it, I'm sure you can marry just whom you like and I should think she would do very nicely...' A sudden thought caused her to pause. 'Perhaps you're in love with Mies? Of course, I never thought of that—she likes you very much, you know, but Willem gets in her way, but that's all right because he's rather taken to me, so if you had any ideas about keeping away from her because of him, you don't need to...'

He was at the door and she couldn't see his face. 'What a remarkable imagination you have! Have you nothing better to do with your time?'

'I'm on holiday,' she pointed out. 'You look very put out, if you could spare the time to go home and take a couple of aspirin and lie down for half an hour...' Her words were drowned in his shout of laughter as he went out and banged the door after him.

An ill-tempered man, she reflected as she went along to the kitchen to put the kettle on, and really she should dislike him, but she didn't. She hadn't forgotten how gentle he had been with the small boy outside St Norbert's and in an offhand sort of way, he'd been gentle with her too. She wondered what he would look like if he smiled and his blue eyes lost their icy stare. She would never know, of course. Whenever she met him she said or did something to annoy him. Somehow the thought depressed her, and even the pot of strong tea she made herself did little to cheer her up.

Mies came in presently, rather cross and tired, which was perhaps why she only shrugged her shoulders when Lucy told her about her meeting with Willem. And when he telephoned later and Lucy told her that he had asked her out for the following evening, all she said was: 'Nothing could be better; there is a film I wish to see and I shall ask Fraam to take me.' She had a lot to say about Fraam that evening, although none of it, when Lucy thought about it later, amounted to anything at all, and she harped on her feelings about him; she would marry him at once, she had declared rather dramatically, and when Lucy had asked prosaically if he had asked her yet, had said peevishly that he would do so at any time. It seemed strange to Lucy that he wasn't aware of Mies' feelings, but perhaps Mies was concealing them—clever of her, for Mr der Linssen didn't strike her as the kind of man who wanted a girl to fall into his lap like an apple off a tree. She supposed they would make a very happy couple, although at the back of her mind was the unvoiced opinion that Mies was too young for him—not in years, that didn't matter, but in her outlook on life, and it was going to be hard on poor Willem. Lucy curled up in a ball and closed her eyes. Her last sleepy thought was of the lovely old house where Mr der Linssen lived; she would dearly love to see inside it.

And so she did, but hardly in the manner in which she would have wished. It was a house which asked for elegance; well groomed hair, a nicely made-up face, good shoes and as smart an outfit as one could muster, so it was irritating at the least to discover herself inside its great door in slacks, a raincoat which was well-worn to say the least of it, and a headscarf sopping with rain.

She had popped out directly after breakfast to buy the fruit which Mies had forgotten to order the day before, and as the greengrocer's shop was in a nearby main street, she took a short cut—a narrow dim *steeg* bounded by high brick walls, with here and there a narrow door, tight closed. It was really no more than an alley and infrequently used, but now, as she turned into it, she had seen a group of boys bending over something on the ground. They had looked round at the sound of her footsteps and then got to their feet and raced off, their very backs so eloquent of wrongdoing that she had broken into a run, for they had left something lying there... A cat, a miserable scrawny tabby cat with a cord tightly drawn round its elderly neck. She had dropped to her knees on the wet, filthy cobbles and tried frantically to loosen the knot. She needed a knife or scissors and she had neither; she picked the beast up and ran again, this time towards the busy street she could see at the end of the *steeg*. It was only as she emerged on to it that she paused momentarily—a shop or a passer-by, someone with a pocket knife... The pavement seemed full of women and the nearest shop was yards away. Lucy was on the point of making for it when she heard her name called. At the kerb was a Mini and in it Mr der Linssen, holding the door open. She had scrambled in and demanded a knife with what breath she had left and he, with a brief glance which took in the situation, had drawn away from the kerb back into the stream of traffic. 'I can't stop here—there are lights ahead—it's only a few yards, let's pray they're red.'

They were. He had whipped out a pocket knife and carefully cut the cord and was ready to drive on as the queue of cars started up again. Lucy looked at the cat; it looked in a poor way and she said frantically: 'Oh, please, take me to a vet...'

'We'll take him home, it's close by.' Mr der Linssen had sounded kind and assured. 'If he's survived so far, he's still got a chance. Let him stay quiet in the meantime, he needs to get some air into his lungs.'

And when they had reached his house, he took the cat from her and ushered her in through the door and into a long narrow hall with panelled walls and an elaborate plaster ceiling and silky carpets on its black and white paved floor, only she hadn't really noticed them then, she had been so anxious about the cat. She hadn't noticed either that she was dripping all over his lovely carpets, her hair sleeked to her head and her scarf awash on top of it. She had been dimly aware that a stout middle-aged man had appeared silently and helped her off with her raincoat and taken the deplorable scarf with a gentle smile and had hurried to open a door, one of several leading from the hall. A large light room because of its high windows, furnished with a great desk with a severe chair behind it and several more comfortable ones scattered around. There were shelves of books too and a thick carpet under her feet as she hurried along behind Mr der Linssen.

He had settled the cat carefully on a small table and bent to examine it while she stood by, hardly daring to look. Presently he had unbent himself. 'Starved,' he had observed, 'woefully neglected and one or two tender spots, but no broken bones or cuts

and as far as I can tell, the cord didn't have time to
do too much damage.'

And Lucy, to her shame, had allowed two tears to
spill over and run down her cheeks. She went hot
with mortification when she remembered that, although he had pretended not to see them, turning
away to ring the bell and when the same stout man
appeared soft-footed, giving some instructions in his
own language. Only then had he turned round again
so that she had had the time to wipe the tears away.
'Rest and food,' he observed cheerfully, 'and in a
few days' time he'll be on his feet again. What are
we going to call him?'

'You mean you'll keep him? Give him a home?'

'Why not? My housekeeper has a cat, they'll be
company for each other and Daisy won't mind.'

'Daisy?' She had been aware of a strange feeling
at his words; could Daisy be the lovely girl who had
been at the dance?

'My golden Labrador. Ah, here is Jaap with the
milk.'

The cat's nose twitched and it put out a very small
amount of tongue, but that was all; lapping seemed
beyond it. Lucy had dipped a finger in the creamy
warmth and offered it and after a minute the tongue
had appeared again and this time it licked her finger
eagerly, even if slowly. It had taken quite a time to
get the milk into the cat and by then it had been tired
with the effort. Mr der Linssen, sitting on the side of

his desk, watching, had simply said: 'Good, two-hourly feeds for a day or so, I think,' and had nodded in a satisfied manner when Jaap appeared with a box, cosily lined with an old blanket. Lucy had watched the little animal carefully laid in it and borne away and in answer to her questioning look, Mr der Linssen had said: 'To the kitchen—it's warm there and there are plenty of people to keep an eye on it. I'll find time to see a friend of mine who's a vet and ask him to give the beast a going over.'

He had come to stand in front of her and there seemed a great deal of him. 'Thank you very much, I'm so grateful.' She looked down at her sensible shoes, muddied and wet. The damage she must have done to those carpets!

'Well,' said Mr der Linssen easily, 'I think we've earned a cup of coffee, don't you?'

Lucy looked at him, noticing now that he was in slacks and a sweater and needed a shave. 'You've been at the hospital. Oh, you must be tired. I—I won't have any coffee, thank you, I was going shopping for Mies.' The name reminded her of their previous conversation and she flushed uncomfortably. But he had chosen to forget, it seemed, for he had spoken pleasantly.

'Only since four o'clock. I'm wide awake but famished. Do keep me company while I have my breakfast, in any case your raincoat won't be dry yet.'

So she had gone with him to a charming little

room at the back of the house. It overlooked a small paved yard surrounded with roses and even in the light of the grey morning outside, it was cosy; mahogany shining with polishing and a rich brocaded wall hanging, ruby red, almost obscured by the paintings hung upon it. He had sat her down at a circular table and poured coffee for her, just as though he hadn't heard her refusing it. And she was glad enough to drink it, it gave her something to do while he made his breakfast, talking the while of this and that and nothing in particular. Presently, when he had finished, she said rather shyly that she should go and he had agreed at once. Remembering that she felt a little hurt, but stupidly so, she told herself. There was no reason why he should wish for her company; he had been helpful and kind and courteous, but probably he had had just about enough of her by then. But he had taken her to see the cat before she went; sleeping quietly before the Aga in the enormous, magnificently equipped kitchen in the basement, and then he had excused himself because he had patients to see and Jaap had shown her out with a courtesy which had restored her self-esteem.

She had thought about the whole episode quite a lot during the day. The house, what she had seen of it, was every bit as lovely as she had imagined it would be and considering that Mr der Linssen had no time for her, he had been rather a dear. She hoped that she would hear about the cat—perhaps Mies could find out for her. She ate her solitary lunch and then wrote a letter, forgetting that she would more than likely be home before it got there, but she couldn't settle to anything. She supposed that seeing the house had excited her; she had been so curious about it…

Mies came home presently with the news that the receptionist would be back in the morning so that she would be free once more, and they fell to planning the day. 'And we'll get Willem to take us to the *bioscoop*,' declared Mies, and then said a little crossly: 'Oh, well, isn't he taking you this evening? I forgot. Not that I care, I see too much of him, he is always under my feet.'

So Lucy felt a little guilty as she and Willem, who was free after all, walked down Churchilllaan to the nearest bus stop. Mies might not love Willem, but she had got used to him being around; he had been her slave, more or less, for years, and anyway, she had said that she wanted to marry Fraam. It was all rather muddled, thought Lucy, waiting beside Willem to cross the street. There wasn't much traffic about, for the weather was still wet and chilly; she watched the cars idly. Mr der Linssen's Panther de Ville or the Rolls for that matter, or failing those, his Mini would be preferable to a bus ride. The Rolls slid past as she thought it, with him at the wheel and Mies beside him. Mies didn't see her, but he did. His smile was cool and she looked away quickly to see if Willem had seen them too. He hadn't, and a good thing too, she decided. Bad enough for her evening to be spoilt, although she wasn't quite clear as to why it should be. There was certainly no reason for Willem to have his evening spoilt too.

CHAPTER FOUR

AT BREAKFAST the next morning Mies monopolised the conversation. She had, quite by accident, she explained airily, met Fraam when she went out to post letters and he had taken her to the hospital to pick up some notes he had wanted before bringing her home. It was only after a lengthy description of this that she asked nonchalantly if Lucy had enjoyed herself.

Lucy answered cautiously. It was a little difficult; she had promised to help Willem to capture Mies' attention and she fancied that Mies wasn't best pleased that he had taken her out, but on the other hand if Mies was really in love with Mr der Linssen and he with her, surely they should be allowed to stay that way? And in that case what about Willem?

'Willem is nice to go out with,' she observed, aware that it was a silly remark. 'I expect you go out with him quite a lot.'

Mies shrugged. 'When there is no one else.'

'He wondered,' persisted Lucy, 'if we might all go out this evening—just for a drink somewhere.'

She was a little surprised at Mies' ready agreement. 'Only it must be dinner too,' she insisted. 'We will go to 't Binnenhofje, the three of us—Papa has an engagement and will not be home; it will be convenient to go out.'

'It sounds lovely,' agreed Lucy, 'but didn't you tell me it was wildly expensive? I mean, Willem...'

'Do not worry about Willem, he has plenty of money, his family are not poor. I will telephone him and tell him to book a table for eight o'clock.'

'I don't think I've anything to wear,' said Lucy worriedly.

'The patterned skirt and the pink blouse,' Mies decided for her, 'and I—I shall wear my grey crêpe.' She got up as she spoke. 'I shall telephone now.'

And she came back presently with the news that Willem would be delighted to take them out and would call for them in good time. 'And now what shall we do with our day?' enquired Mies. 'You have bought presents already? Then we go down to the hospital; there is something I have to deliver for Papa—a specimen.'

Lucy didn't mind what she did; she enjoyed each day as it came, although she did make the tentative suggestion that they might go to the clinic just once more before she went home.

'But why?' asked Mies. 'You have seen it.'

'Yes, but I found it very interesting.'

'Well, there is no time,' said Mies positively. 'To-day is Friday and on Saturday you go home. Why do you want to go?'

'I said—it's interesting, but it doesn't matter, Mies. I've had a simply super time, you've been a dear—you must come and stay with us...'

'If I am still unmarried,' said Mies demurely. 'And now we go out. We can take a bus and walk the rest of the way.'

Lucy agreed readily although at the back of her mind was the vague idea that she wanted to see Mr der Linssen just once more before she left Amsterdam. She wasn't sure why, perhaps to make sure that he was as taken with Mies as she was—apparently—with him. But now it seemed unlikely that she would see him again, not to speak to, that was. Possibly she would attend another of his lectures in the future and watch him standing on the lecture hall platform, holding forth learnedly about something or other. Pray heaven she wouldn't be on night duty.

It was another wet day; she put on her raincoat and the sensible shoes, wondering about the cat. She could of course telephone Mr der Linssen's house and find out. She tied a scarf under her determined little chin and joined Mies in the hall.

The bus was packed and they had to stand all the way so that the short walk at the end of it was welcome even though it was wet. The hospital looked gloomy as they approached it and it wasn't much better inside. Lucy, told to stay in the entrance hall while Mies went along to the Path. Lab., wandered round its sombre walls. Mies was being a long time;

Lucy had gone round the vast echoing place several times, perhaps she had some other errand or had met someone. Willem, or Mr der Linssen? And had it been arranged beforehand? she wondered. She paused to stare up at a plaque on the wall. She couldn't understand a word of it, but probably it extolled the talents and virtues of some dead and gone medical man.

Advancing footsteps and voices made her turn round in time to see Mr der Linssen coming down the central staircase, hedged about by a number of people, rather like a planet with attendant satellites. He passed her within a foot or so, giving her a distant nod as he went and then stopped, spoke to the man beside him and came back to her, leaving the others to go on. He wasted no time in unnecessary greetings but: 'You return to England tomorrow, do you not?'

She nodded, studying him; he looked different in his long white coat; she liked him better in slacks and a sweater… 'How's the cat?' she asked.

'Making a good recovery. He has the appetite of a wolf but a remarkably placid disposition.'

'He's no trouble?' she asked anxiously. 'You really are going to keep him?'

He frowned. 'I told you that I would give him a home. Have you any reason to doubt my word?'

Very touchy. Lucy made a vigorous denial, then sought to lighten the conversation. 'Mies is here— she went to the Path. Lab.'

Mr der Linssen nodded carelessly. 'She comes frequently with specimens from her father's clinic.' He seemed to have nothing to say and Lucy wondered just why he had stopped to speak to her. She tried again. 'I expect you're very busy...'

'Offering me a chance to escape, Miss Prendergast?' His voice was silky. 'But you would agree with me that not to say goodbye to you would be lacking in good manners?'

This wasn't a conversation, she thought crossly, it was questions and answers, and how on earth did she answer that? She said carefully: 'Well, I'm glad you stopped to say goodbye, and considering, it was kind of you to do so.'

'Considering what?'

She looked up at him and glimpsed an expression on his face she had never seen before. It had gone before she could decide what it was, to be replaced by a polite blandness. And that told her nothing at all.

She said in a serious voice: 'You said once that you tried not to see me but somehow we keep meeting—it's silly really, because we don't even live in the same country. I was surprised to see you at the clinic—I never thought...but I've tried to keep out of your way.'

'Have you indeed? I wonder...' His bleep interrupted him and she heard his annoyed mutter. She was taken completely by surprise when he bent and kissed her fiercely before striding away to the porter's lodge across the hall and picking up the telephone there. He was racing up the staircase without so much as a glance in her direction, and all within seconds. Lucy was still wondering why he had kissed her when Mies arrived.

'Was I a long time?' She looked smug. 'I met Fraam.'

Lucy, accompanying her out of the hospital entrance, forbore from saying that she had met him too. For the last time, she reminded herself.

She wondered, as she dressed that evening, if their dinner party was going to be a success; three wasn't an ideal number, Mies could surely have found another man. Lucy, determined to do justice to the occasion even if she was going to be the odd one out, took time to roll her hair into elaborate curls again. And it was worth the effort, for the hair-do added importance to her pink blouse and patterned skirt. Not that it mattered, since there would be no one to see. She wondered too how Willem would behave; was he going to carry on pretending that he was gone on her or would he devote himself to Mies?

She took a last look at herself in the looking glass and went along to borrow the brown cloak again, for she had nothing else.

Mies looked lovely, but then she always did. The grey crêpe was soft and clinging and feminine and, unlike the gown she had worn to the dance, demure.

Lucy, admiring it, thought that it might please Willem mightily.

It did. When he arrived at the flat he could hardly take his eyes off Mies, and he certainly didn't notice her marked coldness towards him. And if he's going to drool all over her all the evening, he'll never get anywhere, thought Lucy crossly, and then told herself that she was silly to bother, she wouldn't see them again for a long time, and by then they would either have married or have forgotten each other.

't Binnenhofje was a smart place. Lucy immediately knew herself to be a trifle old-fashioned in her dress the moment they were inside its door. The younger women were wearing rather way-out dresses and the older ones were elegantly turned out in the kind of simple dress which cost a great deal of money. True, there were one or two tourists there, easily recognisable in their uncrushable manmade fibres, but all the same, she felt like a maiden aunt. She corrected herself; like the parson's daughter. Which naturally put her in mind of Mr der Linssen and she had leisure enough to think about him, for Willem and Mies were deep in a conversation of their own for the moment. But presently they remembered that she was there, excused themselves laughingly on the plea that they had been reminiscing, and began a light hearted chatter which lasted them through the starters and the Sole Picasso.

It was while Lucy was deciding between crêpes

Suzette and Dame Blanche that she happened to look
up and see Mr der Linssen sitting at a table on the
other side of the restaurant. He had a stunning redhead with him this time, but he wasn't looking at
her, he was staring at Lucy who was so surprised
that she dropped the menu and ordered a vanilla ice
cream—something, she told herself silently, she
could have had at home any time and wasn't really
a treat at all. She took care not to look at him again,
something she found extraordinarily difficult because
she wanted to so badly, but it wasn't for a little while
that she realised that Mies knew that he was there,
which would account for her animated conversation
and her gorgeous smile, as well as the casual way
her gaze swept round the place every minute or so.
He hadn't been staring at her at all, Lucy concluded,
but at Mies; they had both known the other was to
be there.

They must be terribly in love. She frowned. In that
case why hadn't they dined together? The redhead
couldn't be anyone very important in his life if he
was so smitten with Mies, and poor Willem could
have taken her out without Mies planning this dinner
and no one would have been any the wiser, and much
happier. For Willem had seen him now; Lucy could
see him thinking all the things she herself had just
mulled over, because he looked puzzled and worried
and then put out. He made it worse by asking Mies
if she knew that Fraam was sitting nearby and when

she said Oh, yes, of course, wanted to know if she had known before they had arrived at the restaurant.

Mies gave him one of her angelic smiles. 'Willem, that's why I wanted to come.'

Lucy plunged into what she could see was fast becoming a ticklish situation.

'I thought it was a farewell dinner party for me,' she said lightly, and was instantly deflated by Mies' 'Oh, Lucy, that was a good reason for coming, do you not see?'

She swallowed her hurt pride. 'Then why not have just dined with Mr der Linssen? Willem and I would have been quite happy in a snack bar.'

Mies said huffily: 'He already had a date, I found that out, but now he can see me, can he not, and that is better than nothing.'

Willem had remained silent, but now he began to speak. It was unfortunate for Lucy that he did so in his own language, but whatever he was saying he was saying in anger—nicely controlled, but still anger. Something which so surprised Mies that she just sat and listened to him, her lovely mouth slightly open, her eyes round. What was more, she didn't answer back at all. Lucy, her coffee cooling before her, sat back and watched them both and was glad to see that Mies was actually paying attention to Willem, even looking at him with admiration. When he had at last finished she said something softly in quite a different voice from the one she usually used when she spoke to him, and then smiled. Lucy was pleased to see that he didn't smile back, only went on looking stern and angry and somehow a lot older than he was, then turned to her and said with great dignity: 'I am sorry, Lucy, that we have spoilt your last evening here. You were quite right, you and I would have had a pleasant evening together. Mies has behaved disgracefully. I have told her that she is spoilt and has had her way far too long; it is time that she grew up, and I for one do not wish to have anything to do with her until she has done so.'

It seemed a little severe. Lucy gave him a rather beseeching look which somehow she managed not to change to one of understanding when the eyelid nearest her winked. Willem, it seemed, was a man of parts.

Mies, of course, hadn't seen the wink. She said softly still: 'Oh, Willem, you're joking,' and then when he didn't reply: 'You are, aren't you?'

He gave her a long steady look across the table. 'You and I will have a talk, Mies, but not now. We are giving Lucy a farewell dinner party, are we not?'

And Mies, to Lucy's surprise, agreed meekly. They finished the meal in an atmosphere of enjoyment, even if they all had to work rather hard at it, and when they left presently, Mies did no more than nod across at Fraam as did Willem. Lucy didn't look at him until the very last moment and then only for a few seconds. He smiled so faintly that she wasn't

sure if he had or not. They went home in a taxi, on
the surface in good spirits. It wasn't until Lucy was
in bed and on the edge of sleep that she began to
wonder who was in love with whom; whichever way
she looked at it, she hadn't helped much. True, Willem had pressed her hand and thanked her when she
had wished him goodbye, but she wasn't quite sure
why, and as for Mies, she was her usual gay self,
only she didn't mention Fraam at all. Lucy wasn't
sure if that was a good sign or not.

She was to return on the night ferry to Harwich
and go from there straight to St Norbert's where she
was due on duty the following morning, which meant
that she still had the whole day in Amsterdam. Packing was something which could be done in half an
hour—indeed, she had it almost finished by the time
she went to breakfast. Doctor de Groot bade her
goodbye at the table, for he had a day's work before
him and was going on to a meeting in the evening,
so that he wouldn't get home until she had left, but
Mies was free and the two of them planned a last
look at the shops with coffee at one of the cafés or
in the Bijenkorf and after lunch at the flat, one last
canal trip through the city. True, Lucy had taken the
trip twice already, but she found it fascinating and
as she pointed out to Mies, it would fill in the afternoon very nicely and the weather was too good to
waste it in a cinema.

The canal boat was only half full and they sat as

far away from the guide as they could, so that Mies could point out the now familiar highlights of the trip to Lucy. 'Oh, I'd like to live here,' breathed Lucy, craning her neck to see the last of the smallest house in the city.

Mies turned to look at her. 'Well, all you have to do is to marry someone who lives here,' she observed.

'I don't know anyone…'

'That is not so; you know Willem and you know Fraam.'

'But Willem never looks at anyone but you, Mies, and Mr der Linssen…' Lucy sighed, 'well, take a look at me, and then think of all those lovely girls I've seen him with.' She added firmly: 'Besides, he's not my type.'

Mies hadn't been listening. 'Willem doesn't look at other girls?' she wanted to know.

'You know he doesn't. He talked about you all the time when we were out.'

'But he is angry with me. Perhaps I shall never see him again.' Mies sounded worried.

'Oh, pooh, of course you will, but I think he'll read you a lecture when he does.'

'Read a lecture?'

Lucy explained. 'And you'd better listen,' she declared, 'unless you're really in love with Mr de Linssen or he's in love with you.'

Mies looked a little shy. 'It would be such a triumph,' she confided. 'He would be a prize which would make me the envy of all.'

'You make him sound like an outsize fish—you ought to make up your mind, Mies.'

Her friend turned thoughtful blue eyes on to her. 'You wish Fraam for yourself, perhaps, or Willem?'

'Good lord, no!' Lucy was genuinely shocked. Willem was a dear, but the only feelings she had for him were motherly, and as for Mr der Linssen...she stopped to think about that; certainly not motherly. She decided not to pursue the matter further.

It had been decided that it would be better for her to catch an earlier train to the Hoek. The boat train was invariably full and it was far better to get on board before it arrived. The two girls had tea out and then went back for Lucy to finish the last of her packing before having a light supper. Lucy felt a vague sadness when it was time to leave; she had had a lovely holiday, she declared to Mies, who had gone to the station to see her off. 'And you must come and see us.' She kissed Mies warmly, 'and I hope you...' She tried again: 'I hope that whatever you decide, you'll be very happy. Let me know.'

She hung out of the window, waving for as long as she could see Mies on the fast receding platform. The station wasn't exactly beautiful, but it was clean and airy and had an atmosphere of bustle and faint excitement and in the gathering dusk of a fine September evening, it looked romantic too—anything could happen, she thought vaguely as she turned away and sat down—only not to her, of course. Anything romantic, that was.

She occupied her journey staring from the window, watching the lights in the villages and towns as the dusk deepened, conscious that she would have liked to have got out at each stopping place and got on a train for Amsterdam. She fell to wondering what would happen if she followed her inclination instead of obeying circumstances; Mies would be surprised but nice about it and so would her father, but she suspected that it would fall very flat the second time round. She would have to go off on her own—she became rather carried away here—get a job and somewhere to live. Her sensible head told her that there were things like money, work permits and an ability to speak the language standing in the way of her fantasy, and it would be more sensible to concentrate upon her future in England.

Less than a year now and she would take her Finals. She tried to imagine herself as a staff nurse, even as a ward Sister, but failed singularly in her efforts to get enthusiastic about it. She went back to peering through the dusk at the placid countryside. But now it wasn't placid any more; the train was running through the busy Europort, its chimneys and refineries mercifully hidden by the evening dark, and then it had slid to a quiet halt in the Hoek station. The train wasn't very full. Lucy waited until most of

the passengers had got out and then got down on to
the platform and turned round to haul out her case.
Her hand was actually about to touch it when Mr der
Linssen's calm voice said, 'Allow me,' from somewhere behind her, causing her to shoot round like a
top out of control and go smack into his trendy waistcoat. 'Well,' said Lucy, 'I never did!' She retreated
a few inches and looked up at him. 'I mean—you
here and whispering at me like that—I nearly took
off!'

She gave him a questioning look and he said at
once: 'Doctor de Groot couldn't get away to see you
off. I hope you don't mind me standing in for him?'

She was surprised but nicely so. 'That's awfully
sweet of him to think of it, and nice of you. Did you
happen to be coming this way?'

'Er—yes, in a manner of speaking.' He spoke with
a soothing casualness which made it all seem very
off-hand and relieved her of any feelings of guilt that
she might be wasting a perfectly good evening for
him.

'Have you got your ticket?' He had conjured up a
porter and handed over her case. 'There's time for a
cup of coffee—it will give everyone else a chance to
go on board. The boat train isn't due in for some
time yet.'

A cup of coffee would be nice, thought Lucy, it
must have been the thought of that which made her
feel suddenly quite cheerful. They walked through to

the restaurant, full of travellers, heavy with smoke and smelling of well-cooked food. There weren't any empty tables; they sat down at one in the window, opposite a stout middle-aged pair who smiled at them and wished them good evening and then resumed their conversation over bowls of soup.

'Hungry?' asked Mr der Linssen, and when she hesitated: 'I am. Let's have soup before the coffee.'

'I did have a kind of supper before I left,' explained Lucy, 'but the soup smells delicious.'

She smiled across at the woman opposite her, who beamed back at her and spoke in Dutch. Mr der Linssen answered for her, falling into an easy conversation in which only a word or two made sense to her, and when he shook his head and laughed a little she asked a little impatiently: 'Why do you laugh? What are you talking about?'

The soup had come, he handed her pepper and salt and offered her a roll before he answered. 'The lady thought that we were man and wife, but don't worry, I put her right at once.'

'I'm not worried,' Lucy said tartly, 'why should I worry about something so absurd? This soup is quite heavenly.'

Her companion's eyes gleamed momentarily. 'We make good soup in Holland,' he offered with the air of a man making conversation. 'My mother is a splendid cook and makes the most mouth-watering soups.'

'Your mother?' Lucy swallowed a spoonful and burnt her tongue. 'I didn't know you had a mother.'

He considered this, his head a little on one side. 'I don't remember you ever asking me,' he pointed out placidly. 'I have a large family, as large as yours. I hope that you will give my regards to your parents when you see them. Do you go home?'

She spooned the last of her soup. 'No, I'm due back on duty at two o'clock tomorrow. I'll go home as soon as I get days off, though.'

'And you take your Finals soon?' he asked idly.

'Next summer.' Their coffee had come and she handed him a cup.

'Ah—then I presume you will embark on a career?'

'Well, I haven't much choice,' said Lucy matter-of-factly. 'I expect I shall like it once I'm in a—a rut.'

'You have no wish to get out of a rut? To marry?' He added: 'To—er—play the field?'

What a silly question, she told herself silently. She turned her green eyes on him. 'Me? You're joking, of course.' She went on kindly: 'I expect you're so used to taking out beautiful girls…they're the ones who play the field, though I'm not quite sure what that means…that you don't know much about girls like me. Parsons' daughters,' as if that explained completely.

Apparently it did. He sat back in his chair, very

much at his ease. 'You know, you're quite right. What an interesting little chat we are having.' He glanced at the paper-thin gold watch on his wrist.

'Unfortunately I think you should go on board: the boat train is due in ten minutes or so.'

Lucy got up at once. Her companion might have found their chat interesting, but she had not, although she didn't quite know why. She thanked him politely for her soup and coffee, reiterated her hope that he hadn't wasted too much of his evening on her, and went to the ticket barrier.

Mr der Linssen stayed right with her. As she got out her ticket he said: 'I could of course give you a meaningless social peck on your cheek. I prefer to shake hands.'

She was conscious of deep disappointment; a peck on the cheek from someone like Fraam would have done a great deal more for her self-esteem than a handshake. She stuck out a capable little hand and felt his firm cool fingers engulf it. 'I've had a very pleasant holiday,' she told him, for lack of anything more interesting to say.

He let her hand go. 'The finish of a chapter,' he observed blandly, 'but not, I fancy, the end of the book. Run along now, Lucy.'

The porter was ahead with her case, so she went through the barrier and didn't look back. A long time ago, when she had been a shy teenager, spending her first evening at a village dance with the doctor's son, he and a friend had taken her home at the end of the evening. They had said goodbye at the gate and she had turned round half way down the short drive to the Rectory to wave, and surprised the pair of them laughing at her. She had never turned round since— not that she had had much chance; she didn't go out all that much. Perhaps Mr der Linssen was looking at her in that same hateful mocking way; she longed to know, but she wasn't going to take any chances.

On board she was ushered into a stateroom with an adjoining shower, a narrow bed and all the comforts of a first class hotel.

'There's a mistake,' she told the steward. 'I'm sure Doctor de Groot didn't book this cabin for me.'

He gave her an impassive look and fingered the large tip in his pocket. 'This is the cabin booked for you, miss.' He added in a comfortable tone: 'The ship's half empty, I daresay that's why.' He nodded to the dressing table. 'There's flowers for you, miss.'

A bouquet, not too large to carry, of mixed autumn blooms, beautifully arranged. The card with it was typed and bore the message: 'Happy memories, Lucy.' It wasn't signed; Mies must have sent it, bless her. Lucy sniffed at the roses and mignonette and Nerine Crispa tucked in between the chrysanthemums and dahlias and carnations; they would make a splendid show in her room at the hospital. She felt a return of the vague longing to rush back to Amsterdam, but ignored it; it was a natural disappointment because her holiday was over, she told herself as she unpacked what she would need for the night before going up on deck to watch the ship's departure.

St Norbert's looked depressingly familiar as the taxi drew up outside its grimy red brick walls and her room, even when the flowers had been arranged in a collection of borrowed vases, looked like a furnished box. She unpacked quickly, had a bath and in her dressing gown went along to the pantry to see if any of her friends were off duty. Beryl, from Men's Medical, was there, so was Chris, on day duty on Children's. They hailed her with pleasure, invited her to share the pot of tea they had made, and adjourned to her room for a nice gossip until it was time to don uniform and go to lunch.

The meal, after the good living in Doctor de Groot's flat, seemed unimaginative; Lucy pushed a lettuce leaf, half a tomato and a slice of underdone beef round her plate, consumed the milk pudding which followed it, and took herself through a maze of passages to the Principal Nursing Officer's office.

Women's Surgical was to be her lot; day duty for three months and would she report herself to Sister Ellis at once, please. The Principal Nursing Officer, a majestic personality with a severe exterior and a heart of gold, pointed out that as several of the nurses on that ward had fallen sick with a throat bug, Lucy's return was providential and she must expect to do extra work from time to time. Time which would, it was pointed out to her, be made up as soon as possible.

Lucy said 'Yes, Miss Trent,' and 'No, Miss Trent,' and hoped that life wasn't going to be too hard; Sister Ellis was an elderly despot, old-fashioned, thorough and given to reminiscing about her own training days when, it seemed, she worked for a pittance, had a day off a month, worked a fifty-six-hour week and enjoyed every minute of it. She never tired of telling the student nurses about it, always adding the rider that she had no idea what girls of today were coming to. No one had ever dared tell her.

Women's Surgical was on the top floor, a large, old-fashioned ward with out-of-date sluice rooms, side wards tucked away in awkward corners and bathrooms large enough to take half a dozen baths in place of the old-fashioned pedestal affairs set in the very centre of their bleak white tiles. Lucy climbed the stairs slowly because she still had a few minutes to spare, and pushed open the swing doors which led to a kind of ante-room from which led short passages to Sister's office, the kitchen, the linen cupboard and a small dressings room. Straight in front of her were more swing doors leading to the ward; she could hear voices, curtains being pulled and the clatter of bedpans coming from behind them. Just nicely in time for the B.P. round, she thought sourly as she tapped on Sister's door. Amsterdam seemed a long way away.

CHAPTER FIVE

LUCY, a hard worker, found her capacity being stretched to its limits; even with Sister Ellis's splendid and uncomplaining example, her days were gruelling. One of the staff nurses went off sick on the day following her arrival on the ward and she found herself doing the work of two. Something, as Sister Ellis assured her, she was perfectly capable of doing, and indeed that was true, only it left Lucy too tired to think two thoughts together by the end of the day. But she had her reward; after a week the nurses began to trickle back from sick leave and two days later, she was given her days off with an extra one added on to make up for the extra hours she had worked. Sister Ellis had given her an evening off too so that she packed her overnight bag during her dinner hour, raced off the ward at five o'clock, tore into her clothes, and leaving Chris to clear up the mess, made for Waterloo Station, determined not to miss a moment of her freedom.

Her mother met her at Crewkerne because her father had a Parish Council Meeting and Lucy prudently offered to drive home. Mrs Prendergast had learned to drive a car of necessity, not because she particularly wanted to and she treated the Ford as an arch-enemy, only waiting to do something mean when she was driving it; consequently she gripped the wheel as though she had been glued to it, braked every few yards, ill-treated the clutch and never went faster than forty miles per hour. Fortunately her family had nerves of steel and patient dispositions; all the same, they ganged up to prevent her driving whenever possible. Lucy took the wheel now, and since her mother wanted to talk, didn't hurry over-much, answering her parent's questions with all the detail that lady liked to have. 'And that nice man who brought you home,' enquired Mrs Prendergast, 'did you see him?'

'Oh, yes,' admitted Lucy cheerfully, 'several times. He lives in Amsterdam and knows Doctor de Groot quite well—he and Mies are very thick.'

She didn't see her mother's face fall. 'She must be a good deal younger than he is...'

'Mies is a year younger than I am, Mother. There's someone else after her, though, such a nice young man, Willem de Vries. They grew up together.'

'He'll find it difficult,' observed Mrs Prendergast.

Lucy said 'Um,' in a non-committal manner. She had changed her mind about Willem, he was a dark horse. True, someone like Fraam der Linssen could make rings round him if he had a mind to, but surely if he had wanted Mies he would have made sure of her ages ago.

'What are you thinking about?' asked her mother suddenly.

'Mies,' said Lucy promptly. 'She's so lovely, Mother, you have no idea. She has gorgeous clothes too…'

'You didn't have the right dress for that dance,' observed Mrs Prendergast far too quickly.

Lucy took the car gently through Beaminster and out into the narrow country road leading to home. 'It was perfectly all right,' she declared. 'You wouldn't have liked the dresses most of the girls wore—nothing on under the bodice—I mean, they were cut so low there just wasn't room.'

Her mother made a shocked sound. 'Don't tell your father, darling.'

Lucy giggled. 'Of course not, but it's quite the thing, you know—I didn't see any of the men minding.'

Her mother shot her a sideways look. 'I don't suppose they minded at all.' She frowned. 'All the same, you must get a new dress before the winter, darling.'

Lucy nodded. 'O.K., but I'll wait until I'm invited, Mother dear, otherwise it's just a waste of money. And there's a lot of life in that green dress yet.'

'There's a lot of life in the old tweed coat I wear when I feed the chickens,' declared her mother briskly, 'but that's no reason to wear it to church.'

'I'll buy a new dress,' promised Lucy, and pulled up tidily at the front door of the Rectory.

The stone-flagged hall smelled of wax polish and lavender mixed with something mouthwatering from the kitchen. Lucy sighed with deep content as she went in. It smelled of home, and hard on the thought was another one; that Fraam der Linssen's house smelled of home too, despite its grandeur. A wave of something like homesickness caught at her throat and she told herself that she was being ridiculous; one wasn't homesick for a house one had seen only once, and that fleetingly. It was because she was tired, she supposed as she followed her mother into the kitchen and then back into the dining room with her supper on a tray.

She spent a good deal of her days off talking, relating the day by day happenings of her holiday in Amsterdam. Her parents hadn't been there for many years and it was difficult for them to understand that it had changed. 'Though the *grachten* are just the same,' she consoled them. 'Some of the houses are used as offices, but they look just the same from the outside.'

'And where does that nice man live?' asked her mother guilelessly.

'Mr der Linssen? He's got a mansion in a dear little side street with a canal running down the centre. I went inside one day—just into a sitting room, with a cat I found—he's given it a home.'

It sounded rather bald put like that and she could see her mother framing a string of questions which she forestalled with: 'Doctor de Groot's clinic is pretty super—he works frightfully hard, a lot of the medical men give him a hand there.'

'Mr der Linssen?' asked Mrs Prendergast.

Lucy gave a soundless sigh. Her mother had the tenacity of a bulldog, she would end up by extracting every detail about him. 'He goes there, too. I didn't see much of him, though, although he's so friendly with Mies.' She drew a breath. 'He avoided me as much as he could; he was always polite, of course, but he told me that he—he tried not to see me.'

This forthright speech didn't have the desired effect. Her mother paused in her knitting to look at nothing. 'Now why should he say that?' she asked no one in particular. But she didn't mention him again for the whole of the three days in which Lucy was home, and nor, for that matter, did anyone else, a fact which she found decidedly frustrating. After all, she had seen quite a lot of him while she had been in Amsterdam, but she found bringing him into the conversation very difficult. She decided to forget about him and busied herself around the house with her mother, or drove her father through the quiet lanes when he went visiting. They were delightfully empty now; the summer visitors, and they weren't many, had gone and the local inhabitants had returned to their rural activities, and with autumn advancing the village social life was waking up. Handicrafts, knit-ins, whist drives were very much the

order of the day. Lucy obediently put in an appearance at a knit-in, hating every moment of it, for she
couldn't knit well and the conversation tended to
centre round little Tom's adenoids, old Mrs Drew's
rheumatism and the mysterious ailment which had
attacked Farmer Will's pigs. After a little while she
found her thoughts wandering. That they should
wander to Mr der Linssen was natural enough, she
told herself; he had been part and parcel of her holiday, and that was still fresh in her head.

She went back to St Norbert's refreshed and ready
for work. And that was a good thing, for there was
plenty of it. There had been no empty beds when she
had gone off duty three days earlier; now, although
four patients had been discharged and their beds
filled, there was a row of beds down the centre of
the ward as well. Five in fact, occupied by ladies of
various ages and all a little ill at ease, situated as
they were in full view of everyone around them. Of
course they wouldn't stay there long, as soon as their
turn came for the operating theatre they would
exchange beds with someone convalescent enough to
spend the day out of bed and retire to the centre of
the ward at bedtime. But in the meantime they sat
up against their pillows trying to look as though they
always slept in the middle of a room anyway, with
a constant stream of people brushing past them on
either side. Lucy, racing methodically to and fro,
found time to feel truly sorry for them and at the risk

of not getting done, paused to have a quick word with them in turn. They were all rather sweet, she decided; the old lady in the first bed was really only there because there was nowhere else to put her; she was a terminal case which stood a small chance of recovery if she were operated upon and none at all if she wasn't. There were those who might argue that she was taking up valuable space when it was needed so urgently for those who had a better chance and were younger, and that she was of the same opinion was obvious from her apologetic air and anxiety to please. Lucy, doing her best to dispel that look, gave the old dear a second helping of supper and a pile of magazines to look at. The girl in the bed behind her was young and pretty and terrified. She had a troublesome appendix, to be whipped out during a quiescent period, and no amount of reassuring both from the other patients and the nurses could convince her that she would survive the operation.

'You'll be sitting in a chair this time tomorrow,' Lucy promised her, 'or almost. Here's Mr Trevett to look at you, he's a poppet and he's got two daughters about the same age as you.'

She attended the consultant while he made a brief examination, exchanged the time of day with his houseman, saw them to the door and returned to go round the ward, checking the post-operative cases and then reporting to Sister in her office. Today had been busy, she reflected sleepily as she went off duty;

tomorrow would be even worse, with six cases for theatre and she didn't know how many more for X-ray. She yawned widely, accepted the mug of tea someone had ready and plunged, inevitably, into hospital talk.

The day began badly. There had been a bad accident in during the early hours of the morning and the main theatre in consequence would start the list late; the six apprehensive ladies would have to wait. It was a pity that Maureen, the girl with the appendix, coaxed to calm by the day staff when they arrived on duty, and the first to go to theatre, should be delayed for more than an hour, for by the end of that time, even though sedated, she was in a fine state of nerves. Lucy, walking beside the trolley at last, holding a hand which gripped hers far too tightly, couldn't help wishing the day done.

The old lady went last and by then the morning had slipped into early afternoon, with everyone going full pelt and getting a little short-tempered what with curtailed dinner, two accident admissions and the routine of the ward to be fitted in. The part-time nurses came and went and Lucy, off at five o'clock, saw little chance of getting away until long after that hour; the old lady had proved a tricky case and didn't return from theatre until well past four o'clock, and then only because Intensive Care were so full they were unable to keep her. Sister Ellis, bustling about with her sleeves rolled up, exhorting her staff to even harder work, took an experienced look at the tired old face, still barely conscious, and appointed Lucy to special her in the corner bed which had been vacated for her.

It was after seven before she was relieved, although she hadn't noticed the time; her patient was a challenge and she had taken it up with all the skill she possessed. The operation had been successful and would ensure at least a few more years of life, but a successful operation wasn't much good unless the after-care was of the best. Indeed, Lucy would have stayed even longer if it had been necessary, for she was sure that the old lady would recover, but she handed over, said goodnight to Sister Ellis and went wearily off duty. She was almost at the Nurses' Home when she remembered the letter in her pocket she meant to post to her mother. Sighing a little, she retraced her steps and went out of the hospital entrance; there was a letter box on the corner of the street which would be cleared that evening. She had slipped the letter in and was turning to go back when she saw the Panther de Ville, going slowly with Fraam der Linssen at the wheel and for a wonder, no one beside him. He didn't see her, nor did he go into the hospital entrance. She watched the elegant car out of sight, conscious that she had wished that he had seen her. Probably he wouldn't have stopped, she told herself robustly, and marched back to her supper and a reviving pot of tea in the company of such of her friends who were off duty. That she dreamt about Fraam der Linssen all night was pure coincidence, she told herself in the morning.

The old lady was better. Lucy, bustling round with charts and checking drips, was delighted to see that, and Maureen, helped from her bed and made comfortable in a chair, admitted with a grin that there hadn't been anything to get into a panic about, after all. And the other ladies were coming along nicely too; yesterday's hard work had been worth it.

Lucy had a lecture in the afternoon, one of Sister Tutor's stern discourses about ward management delivered in such a way that they were all left with the impression that their futures were totally bound to hospital life for ever and ever. Lucy, going back on duty, felt quite depressed.

It was a couple of days later when a notice on the board bade all third year nurses, all staff nurses and as many ward Sisters as could be spared to attend a lecture to be given by Mr der Linssen. It was to be at two o'clock on the following day and Lucy, who was off duty for that afternoon, decided immediately that she wouldn't go, only to be told by Sister Ellis that her off duty had been changed so that she might attend the lecture. 'Because you've worked very hard, Nurse Prendergast,' said Sister Ellis kindly, 'and deserve some reward. Mr der Linssen is an exceedingly interesting man.'

Lucy agreed, although privately she considered

him interesting for other things than lecturing. She would sit well back, she decided; there would be a large number of third year student nurses and they would take up a good many rows—the back one would be at least half way up the hall.

Her friends had kept a seat for her in an already full hall and she settled herself into it. Just in time; punctually to the minute Sister Tutor's procession advanced across the platform, followed briskly by Fraam who advanced to his desk, acknowledged the upward surge of young ladies rising to their feet and then quite deliberately looked along the rows. He found Lucy easily enough, he stared at her for a long moment and without looking any further, began his lecture—this time about Parkinson's disease and its relief through the operation of thalamotomy, to be undertaken with mathematical precision, he observed severely, and went on to describe the technique of making a lesion in the ventro-lateral nucleus of the thalamus. Lucy, making busy notes like everyone else, listened to his deep, calm voice and missed a good deal so that she had to copy feverishly from her neighbours.

At the end, she filed out with the rest of the nurses, not looking at the platform where several of the Sisters had intercepted Mr der Linssen as he was about to leave, in order to ask questions. He must have answered them with despatch because he and Sister Tutor were coming towards her down the narrow

passage used as a short cut back to the main hospital
and there was no way of avoiding them unless she
turned tail and walked away from them. She wished
now that she had gone the long way round with the
others, but the lecture had run late and she was already overdue; Sister Ellis would be wanting to go
to her tea and so would Staff. Not sure whether to
look straight ahead or look at them as they passed,
she compromised by darting a sideways glance. Sister Tutor gave a brisk nod and went on saying whatever it was she was engaged in; Mr der Linssen gave
her a cool unsmiling look which left her wondering
if she were invisible. By the time she had reached
the ward she was quite cross about it; after all, they
had seen quite a lot of each other not so long ago,
enough to warrant a nod, surely. Her small, almost
plain face wore such an expression for the rest of the
day that several patients asked her if she felt ill and
Sister Ellis, more forthright, wanted to know if she
were in a fit of the sulks, because if so, her ward
wasn't the place in which to have them. Lucy said
she was sorry meekly enough and pinned a smile on
to her nicely curved but wide mouth until she went
off duty, when she allowed it to be replaced by a
scowl.

The scowl was still there when she reached her
room and because she wasn't in the mood to drink
tea with her numerous friends, she declared that she
would have a bath and go to bed early. She was

indeed in her dressing gown when the warden, a thin, ill-tempered woman, came grumbling up the stairs. 'It's for you, Nurse Prendergast. Eight o'clock and I should be off duty, heaven knows I've had a busy day.' A gross exaggeration if ever there was one; she had come on duty at one o'clock, but Lucy let that pass. 'There's someone to see you—at the front entrance of the home. You'd better dress yourself and go down.'

'Who is it?'

The warden shrugged. 'How should I know? Didn't give a name, said he knew your parents.'

The vague idea that it might have been Fraam died almost before it was born; it sounded like someone from the village, probably with a parcel—her mother had on occasion sent cakes and such like bulky articles by parishioners going to London for one reason or another.

'I'll go down,' said Lucy. 'Thanks.'

She dressed again, this time in slacks and a sweater because her uniform had already been cast into the laundry bin. She didn't bother over-much with her hair but tied it back with a bit of ribbon, barely looking in the looking glass as she did so, thrust her feet into her duty shoes and went downstairs.

The Home was quiet but for the steady hum of voices from behind its many closed doors. There was a very comfortable sitting room on the ground floor,

but everyone much preferred sitting cosily, packed
tight in someone's bedroom, gossiping and drinking
pots of tea until bed time. Lucy crossed the rather
dark, tiled hall and opened the heavy front door and
found Fraam der Linssen on the other side of it.

She was aware that her heart was beating a good
deal too fast and she had to wait a second or two
before she could say in a steady voice: 'Good evening, Mr der Linssen. You wanted to see me?'

'Naturally I wished to see you, Lucy. I have mes-
sages from Mies and a scarf which you left behind
and have been asked to deliver to you.' And when
she just stood there: 'Am I allowed to come inside?
It is now October, you know, and chilly.'

She opened the door a little wider. 'Oh, yes—of
course. There's a room where we may receive visitors.'

He looked around at the rather bleak little room
into which she ushered him. 'Designed to damp
down the strongest feelings,' he observed blandly. 'I
wonder how many young men survive a visit here?'

She answered him seriously. 'Well, if they're really keen, it doesn't seem to matter,' she told him,
and wondered why he smiled. She glanced round
herself at the upright steel chairs and the table with
the pot plant. 'It is rather unfriendly, I suppose. I've
only been here once before.'

'Was he—er—put off?' asked Mr der Linssen in
an interested voice.

'It was my godmother on a visit from Scotland,' she explained 'Is Mies well?'

She had sat herself on one of the awful chairs but he, after a thoughtful look, decided to stand, towering over her. She thought how alien he looked in the anonymity of the visitors' room. She would, she supposed, always associate him with the lovely old house in Amsterdam.

He took his time answering her. At length: 'She is very well and sends her love. I took her out a few days ago, she looked very beautiful and turned all heads.'

Lucy nodded. 'She's one of the loveliest girls I've ever seen.' She stared across at him. 'Don't you think so?'

'Indeed I do. She made me promise to take you out for a meal while I was over here. Will you come now?'

She looked at him with horror. 'Now? Like this? You're joking!'

'You look all right to me, but change into something else if you wish to.' He glanced at his watch. 'Is ten minutes enough? We'll go somewhere quiet.'

Where he won't feel ashamed of me, thought Lucy, and was on the point of refusing when he repeated: 'I promised. I like to keep my promises.'

She got to her feet. 'Ten minutes,' she told him, and went back to her room. They were going somewhere quiet, he had said. She decided what to wear while she took a lightning shower. The tweed coat, an expensive garment she had bought years ago and which refused to wear out, and the Marks & Spencer velvet skirt with a shirt blouse. She pinned her hair with more regard to neatness than style, spent a few minutes on her face and sped downstairs. At any rate, she wouldn't disgrace a steak bar or a Golden Egg.

Mr der Linssen had other plans. He helped her neatly into the Panther and drove gently through the evening traffic, chatting about this and that. It wasn't until she saw that they were going down the Brompton Road that she stirred uneasily in her comfortable seat. 'Knightsbridge?' she queried doubtfully. 'I'm not dressed...'

'The Brompton Grill.' His voice reassured her, and she was still further reassured when they reached the restaurant and she saw that many of the tables were occupied by people dressed like themselves. Not, she decided, casting a sideways glance at her companion, that she was wearing anything to equal Mr der Linssen's beautifully cut suit. She forgot all that presently; the sherry he ordered for her sharpened her appetite, for she had skipped supper, and she agreed happily to caviar and toast for starters, Poussin en Cocotte to follow and a lemon syllabub to round off these delicacies, while her companion enjoyed a carpet-bag steak followed by the cheese board. And all the while her host carried on a gentle conversation about nothing at all.

But over coffee he suddenly asked briskly: 'And how are you getting on, Lucy? Your Finals are not so far off, are they? Have you any plans?'

She eyed him over the table and shook her head.

'Perhaps you plan to get married?' He sounded casual.

'Me? No.'

'I rather thought that Willem fancied you.'

She poured them each more coffee. 'Did Mies tell you that?'

He gave her a little mocking smile. 'My dear Lucy, I have eyes in my head and I might remind you that I've been around for quite a while.'

It was difficult to know what to say, so she decided not to say anything but asked instead: 'Are you and Mies going to get married?'

He dropped the lids over his eyes so that she couldn't see their expression. His face was so bland that she said quickly: 'No, don't answer, I can see that you aren't going to anyway…'

'You haven't answered me, either, Lucy.'

She frowned and he went on: 'It's difficult to lie when you're an honest person, isn't it?'

She threw him a startled look. 'Yes. You were very rude after the lecture. I don't understand you at all, Mr der Linssen. Here you are taking me out to dinner and yet you looked right through me only an hour ago.' She went pink as she spoke, remembering that he had once said that he tried not to see her.

He studied her face before he spoke. 'I wonder what Sister Tutor would have said if I had—er—greeted you with any degree of familiarity? I thought it best to keep to our roles of nurse and lecturer, and as for taking you out to dinner, did I not tell you that Mies made me promise to do so?'

Indignation almost choked her, but she managed an: 'Of course, stupid of me to have forgotten.' She put down her coffee cup. 'Would you please take me back now? It was a delicious dinner, thank you. You'll be able to tell Mies that you did exactly as she asked.'

He looked surprised. 'Now what on earth?…ah, I see, I put that very badly, did I not?'

Her eyes glowed green. 'No—you're like me, you find it difficult to tell lies. I should have hated it if you'd said how much you'd enjoyed meeting me again.'

He didn't answer her, only lifted a finger for the bill, paid it, helped her into her coat and accompanied her out to the car. Driving back he asked quite humbly: 'You won't believe me if I told you that I have enjoyed every moment of this evening?'

'No, I won't.' That sounded a little bald, so she added kindly: 'There's no need, you know. I think it was nice of you to take me out just because Mies wanted you to.' They were turning into the hospital forecourt. 'Will you give her my love, please? It was a lovely holiday—and Willem—will you give him…' she hesitated, 'my regards?'

He got out to open her door and she held out a hand. 'I hope you have a good journey back,' she observed politely, and then a little rush because she had only just remembered: 'How is the cat?'

'In splendid shape—you wouldn't recognise him, he has become so portly.'

'You were very kind to him.' She tugged at her hand which he was still absentmindedly holding, but he didn't let it go.

'Kinder than I have been to you, Lucilla.'

She tugged again and this time he let her hand go. 'You've been very kind,' she repeated, longing for poise and an ability to turn a clever sentence. 'I must go.'

He caught her so close that the squeak of surprise she let out was buried in his waistcoat. 'I almost forgot,' his hand came up and lifted her chin gently: 'I had to give you this from Mies.'

She had never been kissed like that before. When he released her she stood staring at him blankly until he turned her round, opened the door and popped her through it. Even when he had shut it gently behind her she went on standing there until the warden, muttering to herself, came out of her little flat by the office to ask what Lucy thought she was doing. 'Gone midnight,' stated the lady. 'I don't know what you girls are coming to, coming in at all hours—no wonder you never pass your exams!'

Lucy turned to look at her, not having heard a word. 'It was a lovely evening,' she said, and added: 'But of course, he didn't mean the last bit.' She smiled at the warden, tutting and muttering by her door. 'Have you ever been kissed, Miss Peek?'

She didn't wait for that lady's outraged answer, but wandered off up the stairs and into her room where she undressed, got her clean uniform ready for the morning and went along to lie in far too hot a bath while she tried to sort out her thoughts. But she was tired and they refused to be sorted; she gave up in the end and went to bed to fall at once into a dreamless sleep, so deep that she missed the night nurse's rap on her door and only had time to swallow a cup of tea and half of Chris's toast on her way to the ward.

As the day advanced her common sense reasserted itself. Fraam der Linssen had gone again and probably she wouldn't see him any more, and he had done just what Mies had asked him to do, hadn't he? Perhaps he had pretended that he was kissing Mies. Lucy let out a great sigh and Maureen, having her neat little wound re-sprayed, giggled. 'What's up?' she wanted to know. 'You look as though you'd had your purse stolen.'

Lucy laughed. 'That would be no great loss; it's two weeks to pay day.'

If secretly she had hoped to see Fraam again, she was to be disappointed; he had disappeared as suddenly as he had arrived and although she wrote to Mies later in that week, she took care not to ask about him, only made a lighthearted reference to his visit and that very brief. She didn't mention his visit when she went home, though; her mother, like all mothers, would read romance into a dinner *à deux*; there was plenty to talk about anyway, for on that particular trip home her brothers and sisters were all there too. They all teased her a great deal, of course, but being the youngest girl she came in for a little spoiling too. The weather had turned uncommonly cold too; they went for long walks, breathing the frosty air and the smell of bonfires and windfall apples rotting in the orchards, and in the evening they sat round a fire, roasting chestnuts and cracking the cobnuts they had picked on their walks. The days had never gone by so quickly. Lucy went back to St Norbert's with the greatest reluctance, only cheered by the thought that she would be returning in three weeks' time; she had five days holiday still to come and Sister Ellis, always fair to her nurses, had promised that she should add them to her days off so that she would have a whole week at home. She would have to do some studying, of course, but most of the day would be hers in which to potter round the Rectory, drive into Beaminster for the shopping and help her father with the more distant of his parish visits.

These simple pleasures were something to look forward to; she reminded herself of them each day as she did the dressings, urged unwilling patients to get out of their beds when they didn't want to, and urged those who wanted to and weren't in a fit state to do so to remain in bed for yet another day. The old lady was back too; she had been discharged to a convalescent home, but her condition had worsened and she was in her old bed in the corner by Sister's office, and this time there would be no going to the convalescent home or anywhere else. The nurses quietly spoilt her—extra cups of tea, the best books when the library lady came round, a bottle of Lucozade on the locker because she had faith in its strengthening properties, and a constant stream of cheerful talk from whoever was passing her bed. She appreciated it all, making little jokes and never complaining, and during the last few days, when she was drowsy from the drugs to ease her, she would manage to stay awake long enough to whisper some small word of thanks. She died very quietly the day before Lucy was due to go on holiday, holding her hand while Lucy talked calmly about this and that until there was no need to talk any more. Sometimes, thought Lucy, going off duty, nursing was more than she could bear, and yet perhaps that had been the best way. The old lady had had no family and no friends, she might have gone on living in a lonely bedsitter with no one to mind what happened to her. Lucy, a tender-hearted girl, had a good weep in the bath and then, a little red-eyed, packed ready for her holiday.

CHAPTER SIX

THE OLDER MEMBERS of her father's parish had told
Lucy that it would be a severe winter, and she had
no reason to doubt their words as she left St Norbert's very early the next morning. The bus was
crowded and cold and the sky hung, an ugly grey,
over the first rush of earlier commuters. Lucy, going
the other way, found Waterloo surprisingly empty
once the streams of passengers coming to work had
ended their race out of the station. She had ten
minutes before the train left; breakfastless, she
bought herself a plastic beaker of tea, which, while
tasting of nothing, warmed her up. She had just
enough time to buy some chocolate before the train
left; she munched it up, tucked her small person into
the corner seat in the almost empty carriage, and
went to sleep.

The guard woke her as the train drew in to Crewkerne and she skipped on to the platform, refreshed
and ravenous, to find her father deep in conversation
with the doctor from Beaminster, on his way to London. She was greeted fondly by her parent and with
a friendly pat on the back from the doctor who had
known her from her childhood. Both gentlemen then

121

finished their conversation at some length while Lucy stood between them, her head full of pots of tea, home-made cakes and the cheese straws her mother always kept on the top shelf of the cupboard. She promised herself that she would eat the lot—if only she could get to them.

In the car at last her father observed apologetically: 'Doctor Banks and I were discussing Shirley Stevens—young Ted's wife, you know. She's expecting her first child very shortly and he's trying to get her into hospital a few days earlier. They're very isolated and even in good weather the lane is no place for an ambulance.'

'There's the district nurse,' offered Lucy helpfully.

'Yes, dear, but she has her days off, you know, and when she's on duty she has an enormous area to cover—she might not be available.'

'Where does Doctor Banks hope to get a bed?'

'Wherever there's one in his area. He's gone to London to some meeting or other. He'll try Yeovil on the way back; Crewkerne say they can't take her before the booked date.'

'Poor Shirley,' said Lucy, 'let's hope he's lucky at Yeovil—there's Bridport, of course.'

'Fully booked.' He turned the car into the Rectory drive. 'Here we are. I daresay you're hungry, Lucilla.'

She said 'Yes, Father,' with admirable restraint and rushed into the kitchen. Her mother was there, preparing vegetables, so were the cheese straws. Lucy, with her mouth full, sat on the kitchen table, stuffing her delicate frame while she answered her mother's questions about the journey, her need for a good meal and whether she had been busy at the hospital. But her usual catechism was lacking, and Lucy, who had been looking forward to tell all about her dinner with Fraam der Linssen, felt quite let down.

But not for long; over a late breakfast the three of them discussed her week's holiday and there was more than enough to fill it; a whist drive at the Village Hall, the W.R.V.S. meeting and how providential that Lucy should be home because the speaker was ill and she could act as substitute. 'First Aid,' murmured her mother helpfully, 'or something, dear, it's only for half an hour, I'm sure you'll be splendid.'

'Me? Mother, I've forgotten it all.' A statement which called forth amused smiles from her parents as they passed on to the delights of country dancing on Thursday evenings.

It was lovely to be home again, free to do exactly as she pleased and yet following the simple routine of the Rectory because she had been born and brought up to it. There was no hardship in getting up early in the morning when she could go straight out into the country for a walk if she was so inclined, something she combined with errands for her father in the other parishes, the distribution of the parish magazine and visits to the ladies who took it in turns to do the flowers in the little Norman church. The week slid away, each day faster than the last; the First Aid lecture was pronounced a rattling success, she won the booby prize at the whist drive and spent an energetic evening dancing the Lancers and Sir Roger de Coverley and the Barn Dance, partnered by a local farm hand, who proved himself a dab hand at all of them. She woke the next morning to the realisation that it was her last but one day. On Sunday she would have to go back and, worse, in six weeks' time she was due for a move. Women's Surgical had been busy, but she had been happy working there. Ten to one, she told herself, tearing into slacks and a sweater, I'll be sent to that awful Men's Medical. But she forgot all that; it was a cold day with lowering skies again and everyone in the village forecast snow; just the weather for a walk, she decided, and armed with sandwiches, set off for an outlying farm where there was an old lady, bedridden now, but still someone to be reckoned with. She liked her weekly visit from the Rector, but today Lucy was to fill his place; there was urgent business at the other end of the wide-flung parish and he couldn't be in two places at once.

She enjoyed the walk. The ground was hard with frost and there was no wind at all, although as she gained higher ground she heard it sighing and howl-

ing somewhere behind the hills. And the sky had
darkened although it was barely noon. She hurried a
little, her anorak pulled cosily close round her glow-
ing face, her slacks stuffed into wellingtons. She
would eat her sandwiches with the old lady and make
tea for them both, since the men would all be out
until two o'clock or later; they would be getting the
cattle in, she guessed, against the threatening
weather.

The farmhouse was large and in a bad state of
repair. But it was still warm inside and the furniture
was solid and comfortable. Old Mrs Leach was in
her usual spot, by the fire in the roomy kitchen, sitting in a Windsor chair, her rheumaticky knees covered by a patchwork rug. She greeted Lucy brusquely
and after complaining that it was the Rector she liked
to see, not some chit of a girl, allowed Lucy to make
tea and ate some of her sandwiches. The small meal
mellowed her a little; she treated Lucy to a lengthy
complaint about non-laying chickens, straying sheep
and the difficulties of making ends meet. Lucy listened politely. She had heard it before, several times,
and beyond a murmur now and again, said nothing.
Mrs Leach was very old and got confused; she had
never accepted the fact that her grandson who now
ran the farm was making it pay very well, but persisted in her fancy that they were all on the edge of
disaster. She dropped off presently and Lucy cleared
away their meal and washed up, then put a tray of

tea ready. The grandson's wife would be back from Beaminster shortly and the old lady liked a cup of tea. She sat down again then and waited for Mrs Leach to wake up before bidding her goodbye and starting off home again.

She wasn't surprised to see that it was snowing, and worse, that the wind had risen. The countryside, already thinly blanketed in white, looked quite different and although it was warmer now, the wind, blowing in gusts and gathering strength with each one, was icy. Lucy was glad to see the village presently and gave a sigh of content as she gained the warmth of the kitchen where she took off her wet things and went to find her parents, the thought of tea uppermost in her mind.

It was already dusk when Lucy went into the kitchen to get tea; an unnaturally early dusk by reason of the snow, whirling in all directions before a fierce wind. They hadn't had a blizzard for years, she remembered, and hoped there wasn't going to be one now. The howl of the wind answered her thought and when she went to peer through the window she had the uneasy feeling that the weather was going to worsen. She carried in the tea tray and put it on the lamp table by her mother's chair, then went to find her father. His study was at the end of a long draughty passage and the wind sounded even louder.

He looked up as she went in, observing mildly:

'Bad weather, I'm afraid, Lucy. If this snow persists there will be a good many people cut off, I'm afraid.'

They had their tea by the fire, in the cosy, shabby sitting room, while Lucy made a list of parishioners who might need help if the weather got really bad. She finished the list over her last cup of tea, handed it to her father and went off to the kitchen again with the tray, saying cheerfully as she went: 'I don't suppose it will be needed…there aren't any emergencies around, are there?'

She was wrong, of course; she was drying the last of the delicate fluted china which had belonged to her grandmother when there was an urgent banging on the kitchen door, and when she opened it Ted Stevens, one of the farm hands at Lockett's Farm, rushed in, bringing with him a good deal of snow and wind.

'Trouble?' asked Lucy. 'Sit down and get your breath.' She poured a cup of tea from the pot she hadn't yet emptied and handed it to him, and when he had gulped a mouthful:

'I'd say, Miss Lucy—the wife's expecting and the baby's started. I thought as 'ow I'd telephone from 'ere, but nothin' will get through—the snow's already drifting down the lane and the road's not much better.'

'And Nurse Atkins is in Yeovil—it's her day off.' Lucy started for the door. 'I'll see what Father says, Ted—finish your tea; I won't be a minute.'

She was back in a very short time, her parents with her. 'Lucy will get to your wife,' declared the Rector. 'She knows her way—you stay here, Ted, and I'll telephone and see what's to be done—you'll have to act as guide when the ambulance or whatever can be sent arrives.' He turned to Lucy, already struggling into her wellingtons. 'And you'll stay with Shirley until someone gets through to you, my dear…and wrap yourself up well.'

Mrs Prendergast hadn't said a word. She was stuffing a haversack with the things she thought might be useful to Lucy and then went to fetch an old anorak into which she zipped her daughter with strict instructions to take care. 'And I'll get the spare room bed made up just in case it's needed.' She added worriedly: 'I wish one of your brothers were home.'

They exchanged glances. Lucy, very well aware that her mother disliked the idea of her going out into the blizzard on her own, grinned cheerfully. 'Don't worry, Mother, it's not far and I know the way like the back of my hand.'

An over-optimistic view, as it turned out, for once outside in the tearing wind and the soft, feathery snow, she knew that she could get lost very easily in no time at all. And once she had started valiantly on her way, she knew too that it was going to be a lot further than she had supposed. True, in fine weather it was barely twenty minutes' walk, now it was going to take a good deal longer. But thoughts of poor Shirley, left on her own and probably in quite a state by now, spurred her on. She followed the country road, fortunately hedged, and came at last to the turning which led to the Stevens' cottage. It wasn't so easy here; several times she found herself going off its barely discernible track, but at length she saw the glimmer of a light ahead. It was plain sailing after that, if she discounted sprawling flat on her face a couple of times and almost losing a boot in a hidden ditch. She stopped to fetch her breath at the cottage door and then opened it, calling to Shirley as she went in.

The wind and snow swept in with her so that once in the tiny lobby she had to exert all her strength to get the door closed again. 'Just in time,' she told herself as she shook the snow off herself, and repeated that, only silently, when she opened the living room door and saw Shirley.

Her patient was a large, buxom girl, rendered even more so by the bulky woollen garments she was wearing. Her hair, quite a nice blonde, was hanging round her puffy, red-eyed face and the moment she set eyes on Lucy she burst into noisy sobs.

'I'm dying,' she shrieked, 'and there's no one here!'

'Me—I'm here,' Lucy assured her, and wished with all her heart that she wasn't. 'I'll make a cup of tea and while we're drinking it you can tell me how things are.'

She walked through the cluttered little room to the kitchen and put on the kettle, then went back again to ask one or two pertinent questions.

The answers weren't entirely satisfactory, but she didn't say so; only suggested in a placid voice that Shirley might like to get undressed. 'I'll help you,' went on Lucy, 'and then if you would lie on the bed—how sensible to have had it brought downstairs—we'll work out just how long you've been in labour and that might just give us the idea as to how much longer the baby will be.'

Having delivered this heartening speech she made the tea, assisted the girl to get out of her clothes and into a nightgown and dressing gown and turned back the bedcovers. And it had to be admitted that in bed, with her hair combed and her poor tear-stained face mopped, Shirley looked more able to cope with whatever lay before her. They drank their tea with a good many interruptions while she clutched at Lucy's hand and declared that she would die.

'No, you won't, love,' said Lucy soothingly, busy calculating silently. It didn't make sense; from what she could remember of her three months on the maternity ward, Shirley should be a lot further on than she was. She cleared away the tea things and assuming her most professional manner, examined her patient; there wasn't a great deal to go by, but unless she was very much at fault, the baby was going to be a breech. She had seen only one such birth and she wasn't sure if she would know what to do. She suppressed a perfectly natural urge to rush out of the cottage into the appalling weather outside, assured Shirley that everything was fine, and set about laying out the few quite inadequate bits and pieces she had brought with her, telling herself as she did so that things could have been worse; that at any moment now help could arrive. She gave a sigh at the thought and then gulped it down when someone outside gave the door knocker a resounding thump.

'We're in the sitting room,' she shouted. 'How quick you've been…' she looked over her shoulder as she spoke and let out a great breath, then: 'I didn't expect you!'

'I can see that,' agreed Fraam affably. He towered in the narrow doorway, covered in snow, which he began to shake off in a careless fashion before he divested himself of the rucksack on his back. 'And leave the questions until later, dear girl. Sufficient to say that I happened to be hereabouts and it seemed a good idea for me to—er—act as advance guard.'

He looked very much the consultant now, in a beautifully cut tweed suit and a silk shirt. It was a pity, Lucy thought wildly, that he had had to stuff his exquisitely cut trousers into wellingtons; she was on the point of mentioning it when he asked blandly: 'This is the lady…?'

She made haste to introduce him and then listened to him putting Shirley at her ease; he did it beautifully, extracting information effortlessly while he gently examined her. When he had finished he said: 'Well, I'm not your regular doctor, Mrs Stevens, but I don't think he would object if I gave you something to help the pains; you may even get a little sleep. It will be an hour or two yet and unless an ambulance can get through very shortly you will have to have the baby here. You will be quite safe. Nurse Prendergast is excellent and I won't leave you at all.'

'You're foreign.' There was a spark of interest in Shirley's eyes.

'Er—yes, but I do work over here quite a bit.' His smile was so kind and reassuring that she smiled back quite cheerfully. 'And now will you take this? It will help you considerably.'

Shirley tossed off the contents of the small glass he was holding out and Lucy tucked her in cosily while Fraam made up the fire and then went to shrug on his coat once more. 'I'll fetch in more wood,' he said.

'He's a bit of all right, Miss Lucy,' whispered Shirley, 'even if he is foreign.' She managed a grin. 'Between the two of you it'll be O.K., won't it?'

'Of course,' said Lucy stoutly. 'You're going to have a little doze, just as the doctor said, and everything's going to be fine.' And as Shirley grimaced and groaned, 'Here, let me rub your back.'

She had Shirley nicely settled by the time Fraam got back. He stacked the wood carefully, had another look at his patient and said casually: 'We're going to leave you for a few minutes, Mrs Stevens—just to discuss the routine, you know. Will you mind if we go into the kitchen and almost close the door? No awful secrets, you understand.' He sounded so relaxed that Shirley agreed without a murmur and Lucy, obedient to his nod, slid past him into the tiny kitchen, shivering a little at its chill, made even chillier by the wind tearing at its door and window.

She said in an urgent whisper: 'It's a breech, isn't it? I don't know a great deal about it, but it looked…'

'You are perfectly right, Lucy—it is a breech, at least the first one is.'

Her eyes grew round and so did her mouth. 'Oh, no!' she exclaimed in a whispered squeak. 'You must be mistaken,' and then at his bland look: 'Well, no— I'm sorry, of course you aren't.'

He inclined his head gravely. 'Good of you to say so, Lucilla.'

'And don't call me that,' she whispered fiercely.

His formidable eyebrows arched. 'Why not? Is it not your name?'

'You know it is—only—only you make it sound different…'

'I mean to—it's a pretty name.' He leaned forward and kissed her, brief and hard, on her astonished mouth and went on, just as though he hadn't done it: 'Of course the ambulance hasn't a chance of getting through—I suggested to your father that he tried

to contact the army and get hold of something with
caterpillar tracks; they might get her doctor
through—if they can't then you will have to be my
right hand, dear girl.'

She gazed at him in horror. 'Oh, I don't fancy
that—I don't think…'

'You won't need to,' he pointed out blandly, 'I'll
tell you what to do as we go along. Mrs Stevens
should doze for another hour or so, on and off. Make
a cup of tea like a good girl, will you, for once we
start I don't expect we'll have time for anything. I'll
get the things out of my case—there's some brandy
there too. I thought Mrs Stevens might be glad of it
when everything's over.'

He went back into the sitting room and bent over
the bag he had brought with him while Lucy made
tea again. He joined her presently, accepted the mug
she offered him and whispered on a chuckle: 'I like
the odds and ends you brought with you—practical
even though not quite adequate.'

She gave him a cross look. 'Well, I wasn't to know
it was going to be twins and a breech.'

He spooned sugar lavishly. 'True, Lucy. You
didn't add any food to your collection, I suppose?'

'A tin of milk—for the baby, you know,' she
pointed out kindly, 'and there's some chocolate in
my anorak—it's quite old, I think…'

'We'll save it until we're starving, then.'

She poured tea for them both. 'How did you get here?'

He chose to misunderstand her. 'Through the snow—your father gave me the direction.'

'Yes, of course,' she said impatiently, 'but how did you get here—to the village, I mean?'

'Ah, yes—well; there was something I wanted to ask you to do for me, but this is hardly the time. We can have a nice little chat later on.'

She let that pass. 'Yes, but did you come by car?'

He looked surprised. 'How else? Doctor de Groot sent his love, by the way.'

She re-filled the teapot; it wouldn't do to waste the tea and he had said that there might not be time...'You've seen him recently?'

'Yes—he's ill again.' He added infuriatingly: 'But no more about that; let us go over the task lying ahead of us.' He handed her his mug. 'Now as I see it...' He began to instruct her as to what she might expect and she listened meekly, inwardly furious because he was being deliberately tiresome.

He made her repeat all he had told her, which she did in a waspish little voice which caused a very pronounced gleam in his eyes. All the same, she had cause to be thankful towards him later on; Shirley continued to doze on and off for the next hour or so, but presently she wakened and the serious business of the evening, as Fraam matter-of-factly put it, began. Lucy, well primed as to what she must do, none the less had the time to see how well Fraam managed. Shirley wasn't an easy patient, expending a great deal of useful energy on crying and railing at her two companions, but he showed no sign of annoyance, treating her with a kindly patience which finally had its reward as Shirley calmed down after he had repeatedly assured her that she wasn't going to die, that the baby would be born very shortly and that she would feel herself in excellent spirits in no time at all.

The first baby was a breech, a small, vigorously screaming boy whom Lucy received into a warmed blanket. 'A boy,' Fraam told his patient, 'a perfect baby, Mrs Stevens. You shall hold him in just a minute or two, we'll have the other baby first.'

He had chosen the exact moment in which to tell her. Shirley, delighted with herself and no longer frightened, took the news well and except for exclaiming that they couldn't afford two babies, she made no fuss, and Fraam, bending over her, reassured her with a comfortable assurance that she would undoubtedly get help. 'You'll get the child allowance, won't you, and I'm sure your husband's employer will be generous.'

Lucy wasn't too sure about that; Farmer Lockett wasn't a generous man; it looked as though her father would need to come to the rescue, as he so often did. She heard Fraam say comfortably: 'Well, we must see what can be done, mustn't we?' and felt annoyance because it was easy for him to talk like that; he would be miles away as soon as he decently could and would forget the whole thing. But in the meantime at least, he behaved with exemplary calm, making tea while Lucy made the excited mother comfortable and when they had all had a cup, suggesting in a voice which expected no opposition that Shirley should have a nice sleep for an hour while they kept an eye on the babies.

There was only one cot; Lucy found herself sharing the heat of the fire with Fraam, each of them cradling a very small sleeping creature, cocooned in blanket. Fraam, wedged into an armchair much too small for him, had the infant tucked under one arm and his eyes closed. How like him, thought Lucy crossly and rather unfairly, to go to sleep and leave her with two little babies and a mother who at any moment might spring a load of complications...

'I'm not asleep,' Mr der Linssen assured her, still with his eyes closed. 'Both infants are in good shape and I expect no complications from their mother. I will warn you if I feel sleepy, I have shut my eyes merely as a precaution.'

He didn't say against what, but Lucy remembering his remark—a long while ago now—that he tried not to see her, went a bright pink and went even pinker when he opened one eye to study her. 'You look very warm,' he observed, 'but I think that you will have to bear it.' His glance fell on the small bundle she was holding so carefully. 'I'll have another look at them later on. If all goes well, you can have them both while I get in more wood and forage round a bit. Once Mum's awake it will ease the situation.'

The eye closed and Lucy was left to her own thoughts. Why was he here? He had said that he had something to ask her and that Doctor de Groot was ill again, but surely a letter would have done as well? Or perhaps he was on holiday? Was it something to do with Mies? Her thoughts chased themselves round and round inside her tired head and were snapped as if on a thread when the old-fashioned wall clock let out a tremendous one.

She turned her head to make sure she had heard aright and whispered: 'Isn't anyone coming?'

'Well, hardly.' He had opened both eyes again and smiled at her kindly. 'They'll have to wait for morning, you know.' They sat listening to the howl of the wind encircling the little house and he added comfortably: 'We're fine here for the moment. Close your eyes, Lucy, I'll catch the baby if you drop it.'

She gave him an indignant glance and he smiled again. 'You'll have chores later on,' he insisted gently, 'and you'll be in no fit state to do them.'

It made sense; she shut her eyes meekly, secretly determined to stay awake. The clock was striking four when she opened them and Mr der Linssen was sitting exactly as he had been, only now he had a little baby tucked under each arm. Miraculously they were still asleep.

'Oh, I'm sorry,' began Lucy, to be stopped by his: 'Feel wide-awake enough to take these two and keep an eye on Mum? She hasn't stirred, but she will very soon. I'll have a look round.'

He handed her the tiny pair and stretched hugely and went soft-footed into the hall for his jacket. Lucy felt the rush of air as he let himself out and then heard no more above the sound of the wind. He would, she judged, have some difficulty in reaching the woodshed. She looked across at Shirley, who was showing signs of waking; she would want some attention and a cup of tea, but how to do that with her arms full of babies? She was still pondering her problem when Mr der Linssen came back. She could hear him in the hall, getting out of his jacket and taking off his boots, and presently he came on his enormous socked feet into the room.

He grinned across at her. 'There's a goat,' he informed her softly, 'and chickens. I've dug a path through the drift behind the cottage and brought down enough coal and wood to keep us going for the rest of the day.'

'Where are they?' asked Lucy urgently.

'In the shed almost at the end of the garden. Can you milk a goat, Lucy?'

She said matter-of-factly: 'Well, of course I can.

I'll go and see to the poor thing as soon as possible,
but Shirley's beginning to rouse.'

He came and took the infants from her. 'Good, I'll
sit here—there's nowhere else I can go with these
two—while you cope with her. Let me know if
there's anything worrying you, but if everything's as
it should be she can have them while you see to the
livestock and I get the tea.'

Shirley, now that she was the proud mother of
twins, had assumed an assurance which was rather
touching. Between them, she and Lucy managed very
well, ignoring Mr der Linssen's impersonal broad
back which had, of necessity, to be there too.
Washed, combed and comfortable, Shirley sat up
against her pillows and delightedly took possession
of her family.

Mr der Linssen, taking her pulse and temperature,
congratulated her on their beauty and size while he
listened to Lucy's gentle slam of the door.

'The goat,' he explained to his patient, 'and the
chickens. Lucy's gone to see to them.'

Shirley nodded. 'Oh, I'd forgotten them—there's
Shep and Tibby, too…'

'Dog and cat? I didn't see any sign of them. I
expect they're sheltering somewhere, if they don't
turn up I'll go and look for them. Now I'm going to
make some tea and then we can decide on our breakfast.' He added comfortably: 'I daresay someone will
be along soon, now.'

He sounded so sure and certain that Shirley only nodded; she had her twins and she was content.

Outside Lucy found things rather worse than she had imagined. The wind was as fierce as ever and the snow, still falling, had piled against the side and back of the little house. The path Mr der Linssen had dug was already covered over and she seized the shovel he had prudently left by the door; she might need it.

The goat was housed alongside the woodshed and the chickens next door. She found fodder for the goat and feed for the chickens, then found a bucket and milked the beast before going in search of the eggs. There were quite a few, so at least they wouldn't starve. She piled them into an old basket, set fresh water and prepared to go back to the house. She was shutting the hen house door when a faint sound made her look down; a small cat had emerged from under the hen house floor and was eyeing her.

'Come on indoors, then,' invited Lucy, and started down the path, rather weighed down with eggs and milk and shovel. The little beast darted ahead, looking back to see if she were following, and then sat down outside the door beside a sheepdog, waiting patiently to be let in. He looked cold and hungry, but he obviously belonged; Lucy opened the door and the three of them went in together.

Mr der Linssen welcomed them with a cheerful: 'Ah, there you are. Shirley was wondering what had happened to Shep and Tibby. I'll feed them, shall I? There's tea in the pot, Lucy.'

'Shep went after Ted,' explained Shirley, 'he's that fond of him.' A faint anxiety creased her placid face. 'I wonder where my Ted is?'

Mr der Linssen answered from the kitchen where he was feeding the animals.

'I imagine he's in the village waiting to guide an ambulance here,' he observed placidly. 'There's a good deal of snow about and they might not be able to find their way.'

Lucy drank her tea feeling peeved; no one had mentioned the goat or the chickens. She took her cup out to the kitchen and filled the kettle; the twins would need attention in a little while and she wanted some cool boiled water. She was joined almost at once by Mr der Linssen, who closed the door gently behind him before he spoke. 'Not too good outside, is it?' His eyes lighted on the eggs and milk. 'I see that you've been your usual practical self—you must show me some time.' He poured the milk into a saucepan and put it on to boil.

'What are we going to do?' asked Lucy. She felt cross and grubby and longed above all things for five minutes at her own dressing table.

'Breakfast, my dear. Porridge, I think, don't you?' He was at his most urbane, his head in a cupboard. 'Eggs, bread and butter,' his voice came from inside, 'tea, we have them all here.'

She gave his back an exasperated look. 'I didn't mean breakfast…'

He straightened up and closed the cupboard door. 'Wait, dear girl, wait. So far Shirley is quite satisfactory and the babies are warm and content. We'll take a look at them and get them to feed—if they do, that will take us over the next few hours.'

'But supposing they don't? We might be here for the rest of the day.'

He nodded his head with a calm which made her grind her small even teeth. 'I should think it quite likely, although there is a good chance that a helicopter will get here sometime before dark.'

She felt better. 'You think so? I'm on duty tomorrow.'

He spooned tea into the pot while she stirred the porridge. 'The trains will be delayed and I doubt if anything much could get through the roads.'

'You mean I'll not be able to get back?' She wasn't quite sure if she felt pleased about it or not.

'Do you mind?' He sounded amused.

Lucy didn't answer that. 'The porridge is ready,' she remarked rather more sharply than she had meant to. 'Are you hungry?'

He was busy with plates and spoons. 'Famished. Lunch yesterday was my last meal.'

'Oh, Fraam!' she had spoken without thinking, her voice warm with concern. 'I'll cook you three eggs…' She remembered then that she had called him Fraam and added hastily, 'Mr der Linssen.'

'I don't know about him, but Fraam could eat three quite easily, thank you. Have we more than this bread?'

'There's half a loaf in the bread bin…much more than we shall need.'

He looked as though he were going to speak, but instead he spooned the porridge into three bowls, put them on a tray and carried it into the living room.

Breakfast was a cheerful meal, the infants tucked up and still sleeping while the three of them fell upon the food, and when they had finished and Mr der Linssen had gone into the kitchen to do the washing up, Lucy dealt with her three patients.

It was light now, as light as it would be while the snow continued. She tidied the little room, made up the fire, fed Shep and Tibby again, found a place for them to settle before the hearth and then, leaving Mr der Linssen to keep an eye on everyone, went upstairs to the tiny bedroom and did what she could to tidy her person. Even when she had washed her hands and face in the old-fashioned basin and combed her hair, she didn't think she looked much better, but at least she felt rather more so. Her face was clean and her hair reasonably tidy; not that that mattered; when she went downstairs Mr der Linssen glanced at her with a casual, unseeing look which made her wish most heartily that she hadn't bothered.

But he pulled up a chair to the fire, put the cat on her lap and told her to go to sleep in a kind enough voice. 'I'll rouse you the moment anything happens,' he promised.

She hadn't meant to close her eyes, but she was weary by now. She didn't hear the helicopter, nor did she stir until the cat was taken gently from her lap and she was shaken just as gently awake.

'They're here,' he told her quietly. 'I'll go out to them. Get Shirley wrapped up, will you?'

She already had everything necessary packed in a case, and was nicely ready when Mr der Linssen came back with the pilot, carrying a light stretcher between them, as well as a portable incubator. The twins were small, they would fit into it very nicely. Lucy left the men to get Shirley on to the stretcher and turned her attention to the infants; and that done to her satisfaction, put on her anorak.

'Don't bother with that,' Mr der Linssen's voice held quiet authority. 'I'll come back for the infants.'

She stared at him. 'But aren't we going too?'

'No. Ted's waiting at the Rectory, they'll pick him up and take him on to Yeovil with Shirley and he'll hope for a lift back or get on to a snow plough if there's one coming this way. He wants to get back as quickly as he can—we'll go as soon as he arrives.'

She had no answer to this but bade Shirley a warm goodbye and went back to the incubator. Mr der Linssen was back again inside five minutes and took that away too with a brief: 'They're rather pushed for room, but they'll manage.' He had gone again before she could answer.

She stood in the room, untidy again, listening to the helicopter's engines slowly swallowed up in the noise of the wind, feeling let down and lonely. How awful it would be if Fraam had gone too and left her alone. She shivered at the very idea, knowing it to be absurd but still vaguely unhappy. Shep's whine disturbed her thoughts and she got up to let him out.

There was nothing to see outside and only the wind blowing, although the snow had stopped now. She shut the door and went back to the mess in the room behind her, telling herself to stop getting into a fuss about nothing; there was plenty of work to get on with and if one worked hard enough one didn't think so much. She picked up a broom and started on the great cakes of snow in the little hall. 'The wretch!' she cried pettishly. 'He needs a good thump—if he were here...'

CHAPTER SEVEN

'BUT I AM HERE,' Fraam's cheerful voice assured her as he opened the door and then stood aside as she swept the snow outside. 'Although from your cross face, I don't think I'll ask why you were wanting me.' He took the broom from her. 'The snow has stopped and the wind is lessening, but I'm afraid the lane is completely blocked—it will need a snow-plough.' He gave her a long, deliberate look. 'Now hop into bed, Lucy. I'll make up the fire and then I'm going outside to clear a path round the house.'

She was glad to obey him without arguing, for she was peevish for want of sleep. She got on to the bed without a word and was already half asleep as he tucked the quilt round her.

She awoke to the domestic sound of something sizzling on the stove and saw that the table had been laid and pulled close to the bright fire. She tidied the bed, poked at her hair before the looking glass and went to peer into the kitchen.

Mr der Linssen was frying eggs, and beans were bubbling in a saucepan. He looked completely at home and somehow very domestic. His casual: 'Slept well?' was reassuringly matter-of-fact and calm, as though he made a habit of cooking scratch meals in snowbound cottages.

Lucy, good-humoured again, thanked him politely and asked if there was any news.

'None.' He turned the eggs expertly. 'The telly doesn't work and there's no battery for the radio.' He turned to smile at her. 'Just you and me, Lucilla. Two eggs?'

They ate their meal cosily before the fire and half way through it Lucy remembered to ask if he had cleared the path.

He nodded. 'Oh yes, and I've widened the one to the shed.'

'Then I can milk the goat and see to the chickens.' She poured more tea for them both. 'Do you suppose we'll get away before dark?'

He leaned back and the chair creaked alarmingly under him. 'Perhaps.' He sounded casual about it. 'I would suggest attempting it on foot, but we can't leave the animals, and I don't like to leave you here alone.'

Lucy went a little pink. 'You don't have to worry about me. I would be perfectly all right.'

'Certainly—all the same I have no intention of leaving you.' He finished his tea and went on: 'I should imagine they will get a snowplough through to us and bring Stevens with it; he'll stay and we'll go back.'

'That sounds too good to be true,' observed Lucy, and started to clear the table.

But it wasn't. She was cooking a hot mash for the chickens and explaining just what she was doing to Fraam at the same time when they heard the drone of a snowplough, although it was half an hour before it reached the cottage with Ted Stevens on it just as Mr der Linssen had prophesied, and over cups of tea Ted told them that Shirley and the twins were safely in hospital and that he would stay at the cottage, going down to the Rectory each day to get news of them. He was profuse in his thanks although a little in awe of Mr der Linssen's elegance and great size, even in his stockinged feet and rolled-up sleeves. He wrung their hands, thanked them once again, pressed a dozen eggs on Lucy and walked with them to the snowplough, with old Tom Parsons, who had driven it there, striding ahead. It was a bit of a squeeze; three of them in the cab and Lucy, perched between the two men, was glad of Fraam's arm holding her steady. It was a bumpy, sometimes slow ride and cold, but she felt content and happy. She wasn't sure why.

They were expected at the Rectory; the kitchen door was opened the moment they began to make their way up the kitchen garden path and Mrs Prendergast welcomed them with a spate of questions as she urged them to take off their jackets and go straight into the kitchen where they found a table laden with home-made bread, soup, great pats of butter, pots of pickles, cold meat and a large fruit cake.

'I didn't know when you'd be back,' she explained, 'so I thought a little of everything would do. Never mind about washing and tidying yourselves; you'll need a good meal first.' She beamed at them. 'I've a pan of bubble and squeak all ready and bacon and fried bread, and tea or coffee...' but here she was interrupted by her husband, who had come hurrying in with a bottle of whisky under one arm and glasses in his hand. 'To keep out the cold,' he explained, putting them down carefully before embracing his daughter and greeting Mr der Linssen warmly. 'We are very anxious to hear your news,' he observed, 'we were a little worried at first,' he glanced across at his guest. 'Indeed, before you came, we were very worried about our little Lucilla. We were relieved to hear from the helicopter pilot that you were both in good spirits and safe and sound.'

He poured whisky and then went down the cellar steps to fetch up a bottle of port for the ladies.

'You don't mind if I sit down to table like this?' asked Mr der Linssen.

'Heavens, no—food first and baths afterwards. You'll stay the night, of course—we've put your Range Rover in the barn, by the way.'

Mr der Linssen swallowed his whisky with pleasure. 'You're very kind, Mrs Prendergast.' His glance slid to Lucy, sitting on the table swinging her legs, sipping port. 'I should like that very much.' And when Lucy glanced up at his words, he smiled at her. She wasn't sure if it was the port or his smile which was warming her.

They made a splendid meal, for after the soup Mrs Prendergast set on the table there was the bubble and squeak and everything which went with it as well as the cake and a large pot of tea. She sat at the foot of the table smiling at them both and when she judged they had eaten their fill, she urged: 'Now do tell us all about it—your father has his sermon to finish and supper will be late.'

So Lucy began, but when she got to the bit where Mr der Linssen had arrived, he took over from her, very smoothly, making much of what she had done to help him, until she exclaimed: 'Oh, you're exaggerating!'

'No—how would I have managed without you? You forget the goat and the chickens—why, before today I had never heard of hot mash.'

They all laughed, and he added: 'And of course the babies—I'm not very experienced with infants.'

Mrs Prendergast made an unbelieving sound. 'And you a doctor—I simply don't believe you!'

'A surgeon, Mrs Prendergast,' he corrected her gently, 'and I haven't delivered a baby since my student days.'

Lucy, nicely full of delicious food, was losing interest in the conversation. Mr der Linssen's deep voice came and went out of a mist of sleepiness. It was very soothing; she closed her eyes.

She was dimly aware of being picked up and carried upstairs, two powerful arms holding her snugly. She wanted to tell Fraam to put her down, but it was too much bother. She tucked her untidy head into his shoulder and slipped back into sleep.

'Worn out,' observed her mother, briskly turning back the bedclothes. 'We'll leave her to sleep for a while.'

Mr der Linssen laid Lucy gently on her bed, bent down and deliberately kissed her sleeping face, then waited while Mrs Prendergast tucked her in. 'The darling's absolutely out cold.'

'The darling's absolutely darling,' remarked Mr der Linssen at his most suave.

Mrs Prendergast bent over her daughter with the deepest satisfaction. Her dear plain little Lucy was loved after all, and by such a satisfactory man. She beamed at him as they left the room.

It was quite dark when Lucy woke up and when she looked at the clock she discovered that it was almost ten o'clock. She got up and opened her door; lights were on downstairs and she could hear voices. Fraam would be gone, she supposed, the Range Rover would be able to follow the tracks of the snowplough and there was no reason why he should stay, even though her mother had invited him to do so. She had a shower, got into a nightie and dressing gown and wandered downstairs, wondering about him. He would have been on his way somewhere or other; she hadn't asked and now she worried about it; he hadn't had much sleep…

For a man who hadn't slept, he looked remarkably fresh, sitting opposite her father in the sitting room, with her mother between them, knitting. She stopped in the doorway, muttering her surprise as the two men got to their feet and her mother turned to look at her. It was Mr der Linssen who came to meet her and take her arm. His 'Hullo, Lucy,' was cheerfully casual as he pushed her gently on to the sofa beside her parent.

'You ought to be in bed,' said Lucy, 'you've had almost no sleep.'

He smiled but said nothing and went and sat down again, and Mrs Prendergast asked sharply: 'No sleep?'

'I had a good nap while Lucy cleared up my mess,' he assured her.

'All the same, you must be tired—I should have thought… Finish the row for me, Lucy, I'll get supper. Toasted cheese?' she suggested, 'and there are jacket potatoes in the Aga,' and when everyone nodded happily, she swept out of the room with: 'You men will want beer, I suppose. Lucy, you'd better have cocoa.'

Lucy said 'Yes, Mother,' meekly and went on

knitting, suddenly conscious of Fraam's eyes on her. It disconcerted her so much that she dropped a stitch and decided to go and help her mother.

The kitchen was warm and comfortable in a rather shabby fashion; Lucy could remember the two chairs each side of the Aga and the huge scrubbed table since she was a very little girl. She set the table now and called the men to their supper and watching Mr der Linssen tucking into the simple food with obvious pleasure, wondered if he found it all very strange after his own lovely house. It seemed not; he washed up with her father to the manner born and then went back to sit by the fire while she and her mother went upstairs to bed, sitting back in his chair as though he had done it every day of his life. She kissed her father goodnight, smiled a little shyly at their guest and got into her bed, vaguely content that he should be there in her home, looking so at ease. She would have liked to have pondered this more deeply, but she went to sleep.

There would be no leaving on the following day, that was plain enough to Lucy when she got up in the morning. True, the snow had stopped, but there had been a frost during the night and there was still enough wind to make the clearing of the drifts a difficult matter. The telephone wasn't working and the snowplough had gone off to the main road again and the country road it had cleared was covered once more. Save for the impersonal voice on the radio telling them what bad weather they were having, Dedminster, Lodcombe and Twistover were cut off from the rest of the world. Lucy didn't mind; in fact, when she stopped to think about it, she was rather pleased. And Mr der Linssen seemed to have no objections either. He ate a huge breakfast and then volunteered to shovel snow. Lucy, helping her mother round the house, found herself impatient to join him, but it wasn't until they had had their morning coffee that she felt free to do so. He was clearing the short drive to the gate and beyond a casual 'Hullo' he hardly paused in his work as she settled down to work beside him. It was hard work, too hard for talking, and besides, she only nibbled at the easy bits while he kept straight on however deep the snow, but it was pleasant to work in company.

But presently she remembered something and paused to lean on her spade and ask: 'Why did you want to ask me something?'

Fraam heaved a shovelful of snow to one side before he too paused.

'Ah, yes—Doctor de Groot asked me to find you while I was over here. He is ill, I told you that— perhaps you don't know that he has Reynaud's Disease? In its early stages—he wants me to operate, he also wants you to nurse him. Mies is no good at nursing and after the first day or so he refuses to stay in hospital—his idea is for you to look after him at the flat.'

Lucy stood looking at him. 'But I'm not a qualified nurse and I don't know much about Reynaud's Disease or its treatment.' She went red under his amused look, reminding her plainly that if she had stayed awake during that lecture of his, she might not be so ignorant, but he didn't say that, only: 'I'll prime you well; there's not much to it. But can you get leave?' He added casually: 'I daresay that if I made a point of asking for you, your Nursing Officer might consent.'

She looked doubtful. 'Miss Trent? She might. I've got two weeks still, though I'm not supposed to have them until after the New Year...'

'You wouldn't mind giving up your holiday?'

'I wasn't going anywhere, only here, at home.'

He nodded. 'So if it could be arranged, you would agree? I intend operating soon—a week, ten days, that gives him a chance to enjoy Christmas. He'll need a few weeks' convalescence, he plans to spend it with Willem's people in Limburg.'

'Willem? Oh, does that mean that he and Mies... I mean, are they going to get married? I thought— that is, she told me she was going to marry you.'

He gave a great bellow of laughter. 'My dear girl, I've known Mies since she was in her cradle. Whenever she falls out with Willem and there's no other admirer handy, she pretends she's in love with me— it fills the gap until she's got Willem on his knees again. Only this time he stayed on his feet and she was so surprised that she's agreed to marry him.'

Lucy breathed a great sigh of relief. 'Oh, I am glad!'

He stared hard at her. 'Are you? He appeared to be taken with you while you were in Amsterdam.'

'That wasn't real; you see, he thought—at least, I thought that if he took me out once or twice Mies might mind, but then I wasn't sure because you might have been in love with her...'

'My God, a splendid tangle your mind must be in! It takes a woman to get in such a muddle.'

Lucy picked up her shovel and attacked the snow with terrific vigour. 'Nothing of the sort,' she observed haughtily. 'Men don't understand.'

'And never will. Now, are you going to nurse Doctor de Groot?'

'If he really wants me to and if Miss Trent will let me have another holiday, yes, I will.'

He was shovelling again, but he paused long enough to say: 'Not much of a holiday, I'm afraid.'

'I've had my holiday,' said Lucy soberly.

He stopped shovelling to look at her, studying her slowly, his head a little on one side. 'Are you rationed to one a year?' he wanted to know.

'Of course not!' she had fired up immediately and then went on with incurable honesty: 'Well, actually, I do only have one a year—I mean, to go away.'

'To dance in a green dress—such a pretty dress, too.'

Her pink cheeks went a shade pinker. 'You don't need to be polite,' she assured him rather severely. 'I've had that dress for three years and it's quite out of fashion.'

'But it suits you, Lucy.'

Because I'm the parson's daughter, she thought wryly, and wished suddenly and violently that she was a rich man's daughter instead, with all the clothes she could possibly wish for and a lovely face to go with them so that Fraam would fall in love with her... She attacked the snow with increased vigour to cover the rush of emotion which flooded her. Of course that was what she had wanted—that he should fall in love with her, because she was in love with him, hopelessly and irrevocably, only it wasn't until this very minute that she had known it.

'You look peculiar,' observed Fraam. 'Is anything the matter?'

Lucy shook her head and didn't speak, for heaven knows what she might have said if she had allowed her tongue to voice her thoughts. She would die of shame if he were ever to discover her feelings; he would be so nice about it, she felt that instinctively— kind and gentle and underneath it all faintly amused. She would be nonchalant and frightfully casual, as though he were someone she had just met and didn't really mind if she never saw again. And indeed for the rest of that day and the day after that too, she was so casual and so nonchalant that Mr der Linssen looked at her even more than usual, his eyes gleaming with something which might have been laughter, although she never noticed that. Mrs Prendergast did, of course, and allowed herself the luxury of wishful thinking...

Fraam drove Lucy back on the following day, the Range Rover making light work of the still snow-bound roads, and because he had seemed so sure that Miss Trent would grant her a further two weeks holiday, she had packed a bag ready to go to Holland, explaining to her mother while she had done it.

Her mother had expressed the opinion that it was a splendid thing that she could repay her father's old friend by nursing him. 'Just as long as you're home for Christmas, darling,' she observed comfortably, and Lucy had agreed happily; Christmas was weeks away.

She had been decidedly put out when they arrived at St Norbert's that afternoon, for Fraam had carried her bag inside for her, said rather vaguely that he would be seeing her, and driven off. And what about Doctor de Groot? she asked herself crossly as she went up the stairs to her room. Had he thought better of having her as a nurse? Had Fraam changed his mind or his plans and forgotten to tell her? Was she to go meekly back to the ward and wait until wanted? She wouldn't do it, she told herself roundly as she unpacked her case, pushing the extra things she had brought with her in anticipation of another stay in Holland into an empty drawer.

And nobody said anything to her when she reported for duty, relieved to find that she was still on Women's Surgical. The ward was busy, not quite as hectic as it had been, but still a never-ending round of jobs to be done and she plunged into them thankfully, resolutely refusing to think about Fraam, which wasn't too difficult while she was busy; it was when she was off duty, doggedly studying for her Finals, that she found it hard not to pause in her reading and think about him instead, and worst of all, of course, was bedtime when, once the light was out, there was nothing at all to distract her thoughts.

It was during the evening of the fifth day that a junior nurse came down the ward to where Lucy was readjusting Mrs Furze's dressing and told her that Sister wanted her in the office.

Lucy paused, forceps poised over the gauze pad. 'Two ticks,' she objected, 'I can't leave Mrs Furze half done. Is it desperate?'

'I don't know—Sister poked her head round her door and told me to find you.'

Lucy began to heave her patient up the bed. 'Well, will you tell her I'm on my way?'

Her junior scurried off and she finished making Mrs Furze comfortable, collected her bits and pieces on to a tray and bore them off to the dressings room.

She was quick about it, only a few minutes elapsed before, her tray tidily disposed of and her hands scrubbed spotless, she tapped on Sister's door and went in.

Sister Ellis was sitting at her desk, looking impatient. Fraam was standing by the narrow window, looking as though he had all day in which to do nothing.

'And what,' Sister Ellis wanted to know awfully, 'kept you so long, Nurse Prendergast? Not only have you kept me waiting, but Mr der Linssen, with no time to spare, has been kept waiting also.'

Lucy's mild features assumed a stubborn look; she was overjoyed to see Fraam, but the joy was a little swamped at the moment by the knowledge that she wasn't looking her best. She was tired, her hair was ruffled and her nose shone. Not that these would make a mite of difference to his attitude towards her, so that it was ridiculous of her to mind, anyway. She said meekly: 'I'm sorry, Sister, but I couldn't leave Mrs Furze at once...'

Sister Ellis snorted. 'In my young days...' she began, and then thought better of it. 'Mr der Linssen wishes to speak to you,' she finished. She settled back in her chair as she spoke, intent on missing nothing.

Fraam took his cue smoothly, with a pleasant smile for Sister Ellis and a gentle 'Hullo, Lucy,' in a voice which sounded as though he were really glad to see her again and quite melted her peevishness. He went on to explain that he had spoken both to Miss Trent and Sister Ellis and both ladies had been so kind as to make it possible for Lucy to take the remainder of her annual holiday. 'Seventeen days,' he commented, 'which should give Doctor de Groot ample time to get over the worst. You are still agreeable, I take it?' he wanted to know.

Lucy tucked away a strand of mousy hair. 'Yes, of course. When am I to go?'

'Tomorrow evening, if you are willing. I shall be operating early on the morning of the following day and would be obliged if you would take up your duties then.' He looked at Sister Ellis. 'If I may, I will have the tickets sent here tomorrow morning. I shall be returning to Amsterdam this evening, but I will arrange for someone to meet you at Schiphol and bring you to the hospital.'

Sister Ellis nodded graciously; Mr der Linssen was behaving exactly as she considered a distinguished surgeon should, no familiarity towards her nurse— true, he had called her Lucy, but the strict professional discipline had altered considerably over the years—and a gracious acknowledgement of her own help in the matter. Lucy Prendergast was a good little nurse, one day she would make an excellent ward Sister. She said now, ready to improve the occasion: 'You will learn a good deal, I hope, Nurse; other methods are always worth studying, and any knowledge you acquire will doubtless come in useful when you sit your Finals.'

Lucy said: 'Yes, Sister,' and stole a look at Fraam. She wondered why he looked as though he was laughing to himself. Really he seemed quite a stranger standing there so elegant and cool, it was hard to imagine him shovelling snow and making tea. She found his eyes upon her and knew that he was thinking the same thing, and looked away quickly.

'If Mr der Linssen has given you all the instructions he wishes, you may go, Nurse. Send Night Nurse in to me in five minutes and then go off duty. Goodnight.'

'Goodnight, Sister. Goodnight, Mr der Linssen.' She didn't quite look at him this time.

She had expected to see him again, she had to admit to herself later; she had gone off duty, eaten her supper and repaired to her room, accompanied by a number of her friends, to undertake the business of packing, and all the while she had her ears cocked for the telephone, only it had remained silent and she had gone to bed feeling curiously unhappy. There had been no reason why Fraam should have tried to see her again; the whole arrangement was a businesslike undertaking, planned to please Doctor de Groot—and what, she asked herself miserably, could be more proof, if proof she needed, that Fraam wasn't even faintly interested in her? She tossed and turned for a good bit of the night and went on duty in the morning looking so wan that Sister Ellis wanted to know if she felt well enough to travel that evening.

She went off duty at one o'clock and obedient to the instructions she had received with her ticket, took herself to the airport and boarded a flight to Schiphol. It was a miserably cold evening and it suited her mood exactly.

It was cold at Schiphol too and she shivered as she followed the routine of getting herself and her luggage into the outside world again. There hadn't been many people on the flight and the queue before her thinned as they reached the main hall. She wondered who would meet her; someone from the hospital presumably, but how would she recognise him or her? She put her case down and it was picked up again at once by Fraam.

'A good flight, I hope?' he wanted to know. 'I thought it better if I fetched you myself, in that way we can save a lot of time; I can give you the facts of the case as we go.'

'Good evening,' said Lucy on a caught breath, 'and yes, thank you, the flight was very comfortable.' And after that brief exchange they didn't speak again as he led her to the car park. He had the Mini this time and what with her case and him she found it rather cramped. She sat squashed beside him while he drove into Amsterdam, listening carefully to his impersonal voice taking her through the case, and because she had expected that he would take her straight to the hospital, she was taken aback when he stopped the car and when she peered out, discovered that they were outside his house. 'Oh,' said Lucy blankly, 'I thought…'

'Supper first.' Fraam was already out of the car and at the same time the door of his house opened and Jaap's portly figure stood waiting for them, framed in the soft shaded lights of the hall.

Lucy got out then, because Fraam was holding the car door open for her and besides, it was cold. He took her arm across the narrow brick pavement and ushered her up the steps and into the warmth beyond to where Jaap was waiting, holding the door wide, smiling discreetly at them both. And there was someone else in the hall; an elderly very stout woman, with pepper-and-salt hair dressed severely, and wearing an equally severe black dress, neatly collared and cuffed with white.

'This is Bantje,' explained Fraam, 'Jaap's wife, she will take you upstairs. I'll be in the drawing room when you're ready.'

Lucy went up the lovely carved staircase behind Bantje, trying to see everything at once; the portraits on the wall beside it, the great chandelier hanging above her head, the great bowls of flowers…and once in the gallery above, her green eyes darted all over the place, anxious not to miss any of the beauty around her. She hadn't much time, though, for the housekeeper crossed the gallery and opened an elaborately carved door and smiled at her to enter. The room was large by Lucy's standards, and lofty, with a handsome plaster ceiling and panelled walls. The furniture was a pleasant mixture of William and Mary and early Georgian, embellished with marquetry, against a background of dim chintzes and soft pinks. Left alone, she did her hair, washed her face in the pink-tiled bathroom adjoining, and then spent five minutes looking around her. Even if she never saw it again, she wanted to remember every detail. Satisfied at last, she did her face in a rather perfunctory fashion and went downstairs. Fraam was in the hall, sitting in one of the huge armchairs, but he got up when he saw her and took her arm as she hesitated on the bottom step.

'It's a little late,' she observed. 'Oughtn't I to go to the hospital? Don't they expect me?'

'Of course they expect you. I told them that I would take you there not later than midnight.'

High-handed. She had her mouth open to say so and then closed it again as they went into a very large, very magnificent room; dark oak and crimson was her first impression and she had no chance to get a second one because she saw that there were people already in it: a handsome elderly couple standing before the enormous hooded fireplace, a young man so like Fraam that she knew at once that he was his brother, and a pretty girl who could only be his wife. Her first feeling was one of annoyance that he hadn't warned her; she was, to begin with, quite unsuitably dressed; a nicely cut tweed skirt and a shirt blouse with a knitted sweater on top of it were suitable enough for travelling but hardly what she would have chosen for an evening out. She eyed the other ladies' long skirts as she was introduced; Fraam's mother and of course his father, his brother and as she had guessed his wife, all of whom welcomed her charmingly.

'My family, or at least part of it, happened to be in Amsterdam,' observed Fraam coolly, 'and now how about a drink?'

Lucy could scarcely refuse, so she asked for a sherry and prayed that it wouldn't have too strong an effect on her empty insides, but when it came she found to her relief that it was a small glass and only half full; perhaps that was the way they drank it in Holland. She sipped cautiously, answering her companions' pleasant questions and was relieved when Jaap opened the door and announced that supper was ready.

A rather different supper from the one her mother had produced for them in the Rectory's kitchen not so long ago; pâté and toast, a delicious dish of sole cooked with unlikely things like bananas and ginger and pineapple followed by small wafer-thin pancakes, filled with ice cream and covered with a brandy sauce. A potent dish, Lucy decided, and was glad that she had had only one glass of the white wine she had been offered.

They had their coffee in the drawing room, which, after the restrained simplicity of the Regency dining room, seemed more magnificent than ever. Lucy, feeling a little unreal, sat on an enormous button-backed sofa and talked to Fraam's father; a nice old man, she decided, who must have been as good-looking as his son and still was handsome enough. She felt at ease with him, just as, surprisingly, she had felt at ease with his mother, a rather formidable lady with a high-bridged nose and silver hair who nonetheless had a charming smile and a way of making her feel as though she had known every one in the room all her life. She had talked to Leo, Fraam's brother, too, and his wife Jacoba, and as she got up to leave presently she was aware of deep envy for the girl Fraam would eventually marry; not only would the lucky creature have him for a husband, she would have his family too, to welcome her with warmth into their circle and make her one of them.

She sighed without knowing it and Mevrouw der Linssen said at once: 'You are tired, my dear, and no wonder. Fraam shall take you to the hospital at once—we have been most selfish keeping you from your bed.' And she had kissed Lucy good night. So, for that matter, had every one else, except Fraam of course. He had driven her back quickly, handed her over to one of the night Sisters, wished her good night, expressed the hope that she would remember all that he had told her, and gone away again. She had felt a little lost, standing there at the entrance of the Nurses' Home, but she was sleepy too; she accompanied the night Sister up the stairs to a pleasant little room on the first floor, listened with half an ear to instructions about uniform, to whom she must report, and where to go for breakfast, and went thankfully to bed. She had plenty to think about, but it would have to wait until the morning.

And when the morning came, she had no time. A pretty girl who introduced herself as Zuster Thijn and begged to be called Ans fetched her at breakfast time, sat her down at a table with a dozen others, supplied her with coffee and bread and butter and cheese, introduced her widely and then hurried her along to the Directrice's office.

That lady reminded Lucy forcibly of Miss Trent; kind, severe and confident that everyone would do exactly as she wished them to. She outlined Lucy's duties in a crisp, very correct English, struck a bell on her desk with a decisive hand and when a younger and only slightly less severe assistant appeared, consigned Lucy into her care.

She would never find her way, thought Lucy, skipping along to keep up with her companion's confident strides. The hospital was old, added to, modernised and generally made over and she considered that unless one had been fortunate enough to grow up with the alterations, one needed a map. They gained the Private Wing at last, and she was handed over to the *Hoofdzuster*, a placid-looking woman somewhere in her forties, with kind eyes and a ready smile and a command of the English language which while not amounting to much, was fluent enough.

'Doctor de Groot is in a side room,' she explained, 'he will go to the *operatiezaal* in an hour, so you will please renew your acquaintance with him, give him his injection and accompany him, there to remain until Mr der Linssen has completed the operation. It has been explained to you what is to be done?' She nodded her head. 'So you will know what is expected of you, you will remain with him for the rest of this day and you will be relieved by a night nurse. You will receive free time on another day. You understand me?'

'Yes, thank you, Sister. I understand that Doctor de Groot is to go home within a few days.'

'That is so. Now I take you to your patient.'

Lucy had expected to see Mies there, which was silly, for visiting would hardly be allowed before the operation. Doctor de Groot was propped up in bed looking ill but quite cheerful and talking with some vigour to Fraam, who was leaning over the end of his bed, listening. They both looked at Lucy as she went in, said something to the *Hoofdzuster*, who smiled and went away, and then stared at Lucy once more. She bore their scrutiny for a few moments and then wished them a rather tart good morning.

Her patient grinned at her. 'Hello, Lucy, I'm very glad to see you, my dear. I can't think of anyone I would rather have to look after me. My little Mies is no good as a nurse, not this sort of nursing at any rate. We're going home in three days' time—I've Fraam's promise on that. And now,' he added testily, 'what about giving me my pre-med?'

Fraam nodded at Lucy, not in greeting, she was quick to see, but as a sign that she could draw up the necessary drug in the syringe lying ready in its little dish. She did so without speaking, gave it to him to check, administered it neatly and gave Doctor de Groot a motherly little pat.

'We'll have a nice chat when you're feeling like it,' she promised.

He stared up at her. 'I'm the worst patient in the world!'

'And I'm the severest nurse,' she assured him. 'Now close your eyes, my dear, and let yourself doze—I'll be here.'

She went to get rid of the syringe and then to look at the charts and papers laid out ready for her once the operation was over. Fraam was still there, indeed he hadn't moved an inch, but he wasn't Fraam now, he was the surgeon who was going to perform the operation and she was the nurse in charge of his case.

'Was there anything more that I should know about?' she asked him calmly.

'Not a thing,' he assured her, 'at present. I daresay I'll have a few more instructions when you're back here.' He moved then, going soft-footed to the door. 'I'll see you later.'

An hour later Lucy, swathed in a cotton gown and with her hair tidied away beneath a mob cap which did nothing for her at all, stood by Doctor de Groot's unconscious form, ready to hand the anaesthetist anything he might require. Mr der Linssen was there, naturally, with his assistant, a houseman or two, theatre Sister and a team of nurses, and it all looked exactly the same as the operating theatre at St Norbert's, only of course they were all speaking Dutch. Not that much was said; Mr der Linssen liked to work in peace and quiet; bar the odd remark concerning some interesting phase during the operation, and a quiet-voiced request for this or that instrument, he worked silently, completely absorbed in his task; the division of the sympathetic chain of cervical nerves so that his colleague's right arm might become normal again, free from pain and the threat of gangrene quashed once and for all.

He worked fast, but not too fast, and despite his silence the people around him were relaxed. Bless him, thought Lucy lovingly, he deserves all the pretty girls he dates and his lovely house and his nice family; thoughts which really made no sense at all.

He straightened his long back at last, nodded to his assistant and left the theatre and in due time Doctor de Groot was borne back to his bed. He had already opened his eyes and muttered something and gone directly back to sleep again. Lucy, arranging all the paraphernalia necessary to his recovery, was too intent on her task to notice Mr der Linssen in the doorway watching her. When she did see him she concluded that he had only just arrived and informed him at once about his patient's pulse and general condition. 'His hand is warm and there's a good wrist pulse,' she went on. 'Do you want half-hour observations?' After the shortest of pauses, she added 'sir.'

His manner was remote and courteous, they could have been strangers. 'Please. I want to know if you are uneasy about anything—anything at all. Zuster Slinga will be in from time to time.'

He went to bend over his patient and then without saying anything else or even looking at her, went away.

He returned, of course, several times, to study her careful charts, check Doctor de Groot's pulse and scribble fresh instructions. Lucy, who had been cherishing all the dreams of a girl in love, however hopelessly, did what she had to do with meticulous care and calm and when, later in the day, she had a few minutes to herself, she tucked the dreams firmly away; they didn't go well with the job she was doing. You're a fool, she told herself as she sipped a welcome cup of coffee, and fools get nowhere—stick to your job, Lucy my girl, and leave daydreaming to someone with the time for it.

An excellent maxim which she obeyed for at least the rest of that day.

CHAPTER EIGHT

IT BECAME APPARENT to Lucy within the next day or so that they could have managed very well without her. Certainly Doctor de Groot was a very bad patient, ignoring everything that was said to him, ordering his own diet in a high-handed fashion, and using shocking language when his will was crossed. Lucy took it all in good part, coaxed him in and out of bed, obediently held mirrors at the correct angle so that he could inspect the ten neat stitches Mr der Linssen had inserted alongside his spine, and rationed his visitors with an eagle eye to the length of their visits. Mies came each day, of course, prettier than ever and usually with Willem in tow. She had a ring now, a diamond solitaire which sparkled and shone on her graceful hand. Lucy admired it sincerely and tried not to feel envy at Willem's air of complacent satisfaction. It would have been better if she had had more to do, for once Doctor de Groot had recovered from the operation there was little actual nursing to be done. The wing was well staffed, a nurse could have been spared to look after him easily enough. She puzzled over it and on the third day, when Fraam came to pay his evening visit, she broached the subject, following him outside into the corridor as he left the room. But to her queries he made only the vaguest of answers, saying finally: 'Well, Doctor de Groot likes you, Lucy, you are contributing to his recovery—besides, I'm allowing him home the day after tomorrow.' He gave her a questioning look. 'You're happy? They're kind to you? You get your off duty?'

'Oh yes, thank you, everyone's super. I'm glad Doctor de Groot is doing so well. I didn't know that he was ill, he never mentioned it.'

Fraam smiled. 'No. But he began to lose the use of his fingers and it was noticed...'

'By you?' Lucy smiled with a warmth to light up her ordinary face. 'Can he do a bit more when he's home? He's sometimes a bit difficult—I mean, wanting to go back to work...'

'Out of the question for a little while, but we must think up something—someone from the clinic could call round each day and give him particulars of the cases...I'll see about that.' His eyes searched hers. 'You're to have a day off once he's settled in—I'll get a nurse to relieve you.'

'I'm all right, thank you. I wouldn't know what to do with a whole day to myself.'

'No? We'll see.' He turned abruptly and strode away from her and she went back to her patient, sitting up in bed and grumbling because someone had forgotten to send some books he had particularly asked for.

The move back to Doctor de Groot's flat was made with the greatest of ease; the patient was getting his own way so he was his normal pleasant self, a gentle elderly man with a joke for everyone. Lucy prayed that his mood would last as she installed him in his own room and equipped the dressing room leading from it with the necessities she might require. And it did, but only until that evening, when Doctor de Groot exploded into rage because no one had been to see him. 'Probably the clinic is in a complete state of chaos,' he barked at Lucy. 'Why has no one kept me informed? Why hasn't Fraam been to see me?'

As though in answer to his question the telephone rang and Lucy hurried to answer it. Fraam's voice was quiet and calm. 'Lucy? Can you get Doctor de Groot to the telephone? I'm tied up at the hospital, but at least I can give him some details about the clinic. Is he anxious about it?'

'Yes,' said Lucy baldly. 'I'll get him.'

She gave her patient an arm across the room, pushed a chair under him and went out of the room and returned ten minutes later to find him quite cheerful again. 'Willem is coming round in the morning,' he told her. 'He's down at the clinic now, so he will have the very latest reports. Fraam won't be over for a time.' He cast Lucy a quick look and she schooled her features into polite interest. 'Plenty of work at the hospital,' he explained, 'and his social life is rather full at the moment.'

'Indeed?' Lucy wondered which girl it was this time—perhaps it was the right one; she was bound to turn up sooner or later. She sighed soundlessly and said brightly: 'Mies will be back tomorrow, won't she?' Mies was staying with Willem's family for a couple of days.

Three days went by. On each of them Fraam telephoned for a report on his patient and Willem, when he called, examined him before he sat down to recount the happenings at the clinic. It was quite late on the third evening, while Mies and Willem were at the *bioscoop*, that the front door bell sounded and Lucy went to answer it. 'Hullo,' said Fraam, 'rather late for a visit, I'm afraid, but I've managed to fit it in.'

Between what? Lucy asked herself silently. He was in a dinner jacket, so presumably he was either on the way to or from some social function.

She wished him good evening in a rather colourless voice and led the way to her patient's room. Doctor de Groot was sitting by the fire, a table loaded with books and papers at his elbow. He thrust these aside as his visitor went in and welcomed him with real pleasure, to plunge at once into a series of questions, brushing aside Fraam's enquiries as to his own health. He did pause once to ask Lucy to make them some coffee and when she had done so and poured it out for them both, suggested that she might go to bed. 'We'll be talking for some time and I'm quite able to get myself into bed later on.'

It was Fraam who answered him. 'I'm going to take those stitches out—they're due out in the morning, and an hour or two sooner won't matter. Then Lucy can get you settled in bed and if you still want to talk, we can carry on from there. I can't come tomorrow—I'm operating in the morning and I've a date after that.'

'If you say so,' grumbled Doctor de Groot. 'I shall go down to the clinic tomorrow.'

'No, you won't. I'm free, more or less, on the day after, though; we'll all three go, but don't imagine you're going to do any work. Willem can take over for a week or two. And Lucy must have a free day— after you've convinced yourself that the clinic is still standing, I shall hand you over to Mies for the rest of the day—Lucy needs a change.'

Lucy stood listening to him, not all that pleased that he was arranging everything without a word to her. Supposing she didn't want a day off? No one had consulted her about it—besides, in another week she would be going home again. She would have liked to have told him so, but he forestalled her by asking her where her own coffee cup was and when she said she didn't want any, suggested that she should make ready for the removal of the stitches.

Everything she needed was in the dressing room.

She laid scissors and forceps and a sterile towel and swabs ready and waited there quietly while the two men drank their coffee. When they joined her presently Fraam asked, half laughing, 'Don't you like us any more, Lucy?'

She didn't answer but took his jacket when he took it off and then offered him a clean towel with which to dry his hands. The stitches took no time at all; Fraam whisked them out, laid them neatly on a bit of gauze so that Doctor de Groot might check them for himself, sprayed the neat incision and washed his hands again. 'Shall we finish our talk?' he wanted to know.

'Certainly. Lucy, go to bed.'

She eyed him calmly. 'I can't—not until Mies comes in, she's mislaid her key so I'll have to open the door.'

'I'll do that.' Fraam sounded a little impatient. 'I'll see that Doctor de Groot gets into his bed, too. Goodnight, Lucy.'

She wished them both goodnight in a quiet voice which betrayed none of the annoyance she felt.

And the next morning Doctor de Groot told her happily that Fraam would be calling for them the following morning and could she be ready by ten o'clock. 'A brief visit to the clinic,' he explained airily, 'and then you are to have the rest of the day to yourself. Mies will come for me in a taxi.'

'When?'

'Oh, don't worry, you will be able to see me safely into it before you go off.'

'But Doctor de Groot, I'm not sure that I want to have a day off—I've no plans.'

He waved a vague hand. 'Plans? What does a young thing like you want with plàns? All Amsterdam before you and you want plans! Go out and enjoy yourself—have you any money, my dear?'

'Yes, thank you, enough for a meal and that sort of thing.'

'Ah, good. If it's not too cold outside, we'll walk to the corner and back, shall we?'

She had both of them ready by ten o'clock, Doctor de Groot well muffled against the chilly wind and herself buttoned into her winter coat. She was wearing a sensible pair of shoes too; if she was to spend the day walking around the city, she had better have comfortable feet. 'What time shall I come back?' she asked.

'Any time you like, Lucy—take a key and let yourself in.'

She had a clear mental picture of herself filling in the evening hours with a cinema and then eating a *broodje* as slowly as possible. She hadn't enough money to go to a restaurant and she wasn't sure that she wanted to even if she had.

Fraam was punctual, driving the Rolls so that the doctor should have a comfortable ride. Mies had gone on ahead, for she had continued to work while her father was ill, but she would leave early that day in order to go back home with him. She had been a little mysterious when she had told Lucy the evening before, but Lucy hadn't asked questions; it would be something to do with Willem, she supposed.

The clinic was crowded with patients. Fraam, leading the way down the passage to Doctor de Groot's room, sat him in his chair and said: 'You may have half an hour.'

'My dear Fraam, what can I do in that short time?'

'Nothing much, that's why I said half an hour. Longer tomorrow, perhaps. Now, what do you want to do first? See Willem—Jo's here, too, and so is Doctor Fiske.'

'Willem and Fiske, then. What about you?'

'I'll see a couple of patients while I'm here.' Fraam's eyes slid to Lucy, standing between them. 'Will you wait for half an hour, Lucy? Perhaps with Mies.'

She couldn't really see why she had to wait. There were plenty of people to see the doctor back to his house; on the other hand, there would be less day to get through... She nodded and went to find Mies and give her a hand with the patients' files.

It seemed less than half an hour when Fraam put his head round the door: 'Mies, your father's ready to leave.' He had his own coat on again, too, so presumably he was driving them back after all. Lucy got up too and went to the door with Mies, to find a taxi there and Doctor de Groot already in it. He called cheerfully to her as Mies got in and she smiled and waved and then turned away to start walking into the city. Mies had said it wasn't a very nice part for a girl to walk alone, but she wasn't worried about that.

Fraam's hand on her arm stopped her before she had gone ten yards.

'Wrong way,' he observed blandly, 'the car's over here.'

'I should like to walk,' she told him, 'thank you all the same.'

'So you shall, but I can't leave the car here, I'll take it home and we can start walking from there.'

'We?' she asked weakly.

'I told you that I had a day off.'

'Yes—but...'

'Well, we're going to spend it together.'

It didn't make sense. 'It's very kind of you,' she began, 'but there's no need. I mean, I don't suppose you get many days off and it's a pity to waste one.'

'Why should I be wasting it?' He sounded amused, standing there on the pavement, looking down at her.

'Well,' she began once more, 'with me, you know.'

There was no one about, the bleak street was empty of everything but the wind, the shabby buildings around them presented blind fronts. Fraam bent down and kissed her very gently. 'For a parson's daughter,' he said in a gentle voice to melt her very bones, 'you talk a great deal of nonsense.' He took her arm and stuffed her just as gently into the Rolls and got in beside her. 'I'm going to marry you,' he told her. 'You can think about it on the way to the house.'

Of course she thought about it, but not coherently. Thoughts tumbled and jostled themselves round her head and none of them made sense. They were halfway there before she ventured without looking at him: 'Why?'

'We'll come to that later.'

'Yes, but—but I thought—there's a girl called Eloise...' She paused to think. 'And that lovely girl who was in the car when the little boy ran across the road...'

'For the life of me I can't remember her name. She was just a girl, Lucy, like quite a few others. Eloise too.' He allowed the Rolls to sigh to a dignified halt before his house and turned to look at her. 'Do you mind?'

'No, not in the least.' A whopping great lie; she minded very much, she was, she discovered, fiercely jealous of each and every one of them.

'No? I'm disappointed, I hoped that you would mind very much.' He didn't sound in the least disappointed.

Jaap had the door open and his dignified smile held a welcome. 'Coffee is in the small sitting room,' he informed them, and led the way across the hall to throw open a door. Lucy, following him, thought that Fraam must be one of the few people left in the world whose servants treated him as though he were something to be cherished.

The room was small and extremely comfortably furnished with deep velvet-covered chairs and sofas in a rich plum colour. The walls were white and hung with paintings—lovely flower paintings, delicately done. There was a fire burning in the small marble fireplace and as they went in a stout, fresh-faced girl brought in the coffee tray.

'Take off that coat,' suggested Fraam, 'and sit over here by the fire.' He had flung his own coat down as they had entered the hall and she put hers tidily over the back of a chair and sat down, wishing she was wearing something smarter than the tweed skirt and woolly sweater she had considered good enough for her day out.

She was feeling awkward too, although it was obvious that Fraam was perfectly at ease. He gave her her coffee and began to discuss what they should do with their day, but only to put her at her ease, for presently he said: 'Supposing we don't do any sight-seeing and go to my mother's for lunch?'

She choked a little on her coffee. 'Your mother? But does she...where does she live?' She tried to sound cool while all the while all she wanted to do was to fling down her delicate coffee cup and beg him to explain—there must be some reason why he wanted to marry her, he couldn't love her, and surely she wasn't the kind of girl with whom a man got infatuated? Perhaps she was a change from all the lovely creatures she had seen him with?

She heard him laugh softly. 'You're not listening and I can read every thought in your face, Lucy. Mother lives in Wassenaar. If you like, we'll have lunch with her and my father and then go for a walk—there's miles of beach—it's empty at this time of year.' He got up to fill her coffee cup. 'You don't believe me, do you? Perhaps when we've had our walk, you will.'

They set out half an hour later, Fraam chatting easily about nothing that mattered and Lucy almost silent, a dozen questions on her tongue and not daring to utter one of them.

Fraam's parents had a house by the sea, with the golf course behind the house and the wide sands only a few hundred yards away. The house was large and Edwardian in style, with a great many small windows and balconies and a roof which arched itself over them like eyebrows. It was encircled by a large garden, very neat and bare now that winter was upon them, but behind the flower beds there were a great many trees, sheltering it from the stares of anyone on the road. Lucy, who still hadn't found her tongue, crossed the well raked gravel beside Fraam and when he opened the door beneath a heavy arch, went past

him into a square lobby. They were met here by a
bustling elderly woman who opened the inner door
for them, made some laughing rejoinder to Fraam's
greeting and then smiled at Lucy. 'This is Ton—she
housekeeps for my mother. If you like to go with her
you can leave your coat.'

He spoke in a friendly way, but there was nothing
warmer in his manner than that; Lucy, following Ton
across the hall to a small cloakroom, began to wonder if she had dreamt their conversation. She still
looked bewildered when she returned to where he
was waiting for her in the hall, but it hadn't been a
dream; he bent and kissed her hard before taking her
arm and ushering her down a short passage and into
a room at the side of the house. It was high-ceilinged,
as most Dutch houses are, with a heavily embossed
hanging on the walls, a richly coloured carpet cov-
ering most of the parquet floor and some quite beautiful William and Mary furniture.

Fraam's parents were there, standing at one of the
big windows looking out over the garden, but they
turned as they went in and came forward to greet
them, looking not in the least surprised. And although nothing was said either then or during the
lunch they presently ate, she couldn't fail to see that
she was regarded as part of the family, so that presently, walking briskly along the hard sand with
Fraam, she was emboldened to ask: 'Do your parents

know—about—well, about you asking me to marry you?'

He had tucked a hand under her arm, steadying her against the wind. 'Oh, yes—I mentioned it some time ago.'

She turned her head to look at him. 'Some time ago? But you never said…' She trailed off into silence, and watched him smile.

'No. I had to wait for the right moment, didn't I?' He stopped and turned her round to face him. 'And perhaps this is the right moment for you to give me your answer.'

He hadn't said that he loved her, had he? But he wanted to marry her. She would make him a good wife; she was sure of that because she loved him. She put up a hand to tuck in a strand of hair the wind had whipped loose.

'Yes, I'll marry you, Fraam. I'm—I'm still surprised about it, but I'm quite sure.'

'Why are you sure, dear girl?'

She met his steady gaze without affectation. 'I love you, Fraam; I didn't know until that day we were shovelling snow…'

'I know, Lucy.' His voice was very gentle.

She looked at him, startled. 'Oh, did you? How?'

He had pulled her close. 'I'm a mind-reader, especially when it comes to you.' He kissed her slowly. 'We'll marry soon, Lucy—there's no reason why we shouldn't, is there?'

She rubbed her cheek against the thick wool of his coat. 'Yes, there is. I have to give a month's notice.'

'I'll settle that,' he told her carelessly. 'You won't need to go back to St Norbert's.'

'Oh, but I must—I mean, it will all have to be explained.' She frowned a little. 'I can't just walk out.'

'We'll sort that out later on.' Fraam started to walk again, his arm round her shoulders. 'We'll telephone your mother and father when we go back.'

'They'll be surprised.'

He said on a laugh: 'Your mother won't.' And then: 'You'll be able to leave Doctor de Groot in a couple of days and come to my house until we can go back to England—I've several cases coming up, I'm afraid…'

'Oh, but I can't do that!'

She felt his hand tighten on her shoulder. 'You haven't met my young sister yet, have you? She's coming to pay me a visit—you'll enjoy getting to know her.'

'Oh,' said Lucy again, 'well, yes, I shall.' The wind was in their faces now and the seashore looked bleak and grey under the wintry sky—the bad weather had come early, there had been no mild days for quite a while. She was cold even in her winter coat but so happy that she hardly felt it. None of it seemed real, of course; just a lovely dream which could shatter and become her mundane life once

more with no Fraam in it. 'I can't think why...' she
began, and caught her breath.

'You're still scared, aren't you? When you're quite
used to the idea, I'll tell you why.' He smiled so
kindly that she felt a lump in her throat. 'Mama
wanted us to stay for dinner, but I thought we would
go somewhere and dine together. Would you like
that?'

Lucy nodded and then frowned. 'I'm not dressed
for going out.'

'You look perfectly all right to me—we'll go to
Dikker and Thijs, it'll be quiet at this time of year,
we can stay as long as we like.'

It was a lovely evening. Lucy, lying wide awake
in bed that night, went over every second of it, fin-
gering the magnificent ruby and diamond ring on her
finger. Fraam had taken it from his pocket during the
evening and put it there and by some good chance it
had fitted perfectly. It was old, he had explained, left
to him by his grandmother when he had been a very
young man; he had promised himself then that he
would keep it until he could put it on the hand of
the girl he was going to marry. Lucy sat up in bed
and turned the light on just to have another look at
it. It was so beautiful that she left the light on and
sat up against her pillows and went on thinking about
the evening.

Fraam's parents had been kind. They had welcomed her into the family with just the right kind of

remarks, told her that she was to come and see them again as soon as possible and expressed their delight at the idea of having her for a daughter-in-law. And Fraam had been a dear. She repeated that to herself because right at the back of her mind was the vague thought that he still hadn't said that he loved her and his manner, although flatteringly attentive, had been almost like that of an old friend, not a man who had just proposed. She wanted too much, she told herself; more than likely she wasn't a girl to inspire that kind of feeling in a man. It was surely enough that he wanted her for his wife. She went to sleep on the thought and by morning her doubts had dwindled to mere wisps in her mind.

Mies was flatteringly impressed but disconcertingly surprised too. She exclaimed with unthinking frankness: 'I am amazed, Lucy—Fraam has had eyes only for Adilia, who is beautiful—when you returned to England he took her out many times. What will your parents say?'

'They're delighted.' Lucy tried to speak lightly, but she frowned as she spoke. Here was a new name and a new girl. 'Adilia—I don't think I've heard about her. Did I ever meet her?'

Mies thought. 'Fraam danced with her at the hospital ball, she was wearing a flame-coloured dress, very chic. They've known each other for ages. I quite thought...' She looked at Lucy's face and added brightly: 'But that means nothing; he has had so many girl-friends, but Adilia he sees more than the others. But not of course now that he is engaged to you.' She added hastily: 'You must not be worried.'

'I'm not in the least worried,' declared Lucy, consumed with enough worry to sink her. She would ask Fraam; he would probably see her during the day. She cheered up at the thought and went along to see how Doctor de Groot was and to break the news to him. He wasn't in the least surprised, indeed he suggested that she might like to leave then and there. 'I'm quite able to look after myself,' he told her, 'and Fraam did mention something about his sister paying him a visit—I daresay he plans for you to go and stay with him while she's there.'

'Well, yes, he does. But don't you want me here? I never did have much to do, I know, but you're not going back to work yet...'

He looked benignly at her. 'Just an hour each day,' he murmured. 'I've already discussed it with Fraam—I'll go away for Christmas as I said I would, but I just want to keep my hand in. Now run along, my dear, I daresay Fraam will be along to see you.'

But Fraam didn't come—he telephoned at lunch time to say that he wouldn't be able to get away but could she be ready if he called for her after breakfast the next day? He sounded remote and cool, and Lucy, anxious for her world to be quite perfect, put that down to pressure of work and perhaps other people listening to him telephoning. All the same, she thought wistfully, he could have called her dear just once. She shook her head to rid it of the doubts which kept filling it; just because Mies had told her about Adilia; probably it was all hot air...

She was ready and waiting when he arrived the next morning and his hard, urgent kiss was more than she had expected—a great deal more, she decided happily as they made their farewells and she got into the Mini beside him. Mies must have got it all wrong about Adilia. She responded to Fraam's easy conversation with a lightheartedness which gave her a happy glow.

His sister came into the hall the moment they entered the house and before Fraam could speak volunteered the information that her name was Lisabertha, that she was delighted to meet Lucy, that they were almost the same age and that she was quite positive that they would be the firmest of friends. She paused just long enough to give Lucy a hug and then threw her arms round her brother's neck. 'Dear Fraam,' she declared, 'isn't this fun? And may I ask Rob to dinner this evening?' She turned to Lucy. 'I'm going to marry him next year,' she told her. 'He works in Utrecht, but he said he could get here by seven o'clock.'

Fraam chuckled. 'So he's already been asked to dinner?' He smiled at Lucy. 'If you two like to go into the sitting room I'll get Jaap to take the cases up.'

He stayed and had coffee with them and then left them to their own devices with the remark that he had work to do and would see them that evening. Lucy, who would have liked to have been kissed again, got a friendly smile, that was all.

The day passed very pleasantly. Lisabertha was obviously the darling of her family and had a great fondness for her eldest brother; she talked about him for a good deal of the time and Lucy listened to every word, filling in the gaps about him with interesting titbits of information. He had been in love several times, his young sister informed her, but never seriously. They had all begun to think that he would never marry, and now here was dear Lucy, and how glad they were. Where had they met and when was the wedding to be and what was Lucy going to wear? To all of which Lucy gave vague replies. Their meeting had been most unglamorous and the less said about it the better, she decided, and she had no idea when they were to marry. Fraam had suggested that she left the hospital at once, but at the back of her mind she wasn't too sure about that. Supposing he were to change his mind? If she worked for another month, that would give him time to be quite sure. But even as she thought it, the other half of her mind was denying it. Fraam wasn't a man to change his mind.

Certainly there was nothing in his manner to give her any cause for doubt that evening. The three of them dined together and then sat round the fire in the drawing room, talking idly, until Lisabertha declared that she was going to bed, and when Lucy said that she would go too, Fraam begged her to stay a little longer. 'For I have hardly seen you,' he protested, 'and we have so much to discuss.'

But the discussion, it turned out, wasn't quite what she had expected: whether they should visit his parents on the following day or the one after, and had she any preference as to when she returned to England.

'Well, I hadn't thought about it,' said Lucy. 'If I give a month's notice I suppose the quicker I go back to St Norbert's the better.'

He frowned. 'You seem determined to do that,' he observed rather coldly. 'I told you that it could be arranged that you left at any time...' He got up and strolled over to the window and looked out into the dark night, holding back the heavy curtains. 'You are not anxious to marry me as soon as possible, then, Lucy?'

'Yes—well, no. It's...' she paused, at a loss for words. 'I mean, supposing you changed your mind and it would be too late.'

'You think that I might change my mind?' His voice was silky.

It seemed a good opportunity to take the bull by the horns. 'I'm not at all the kind of girl everyone expected you to marry; Mies said, and so did Lisabertha, that you liked pretty girls—not like me at all.' She drew a little breath and asked in a rush: 'Who is Adilia?'

He didn't answer her for a long moment but stood by the window still, staring at her. Finally he said: 'I have rushed things too fast, I believe. You are uncertain of me, Lucy—indeed, possibly you don't quite trust me. I will tell you who Adilia is and then we will forget this whole conversation and return to our former pleasant task of getting to know each other. She is a girl I have known for some years; I have never had any wish to marry her, just as I have never had any wish to marry any of the girls I have taken out from time to time.'

He walked over to her and pulled her gently to her feet. 'I have never asked anyone to marry me before, Lucy.' He bent and kissed her lightly. 'Go to bed, my dear. I wish I had all day to spend with you tomorrow, but I'm not free until the late afternoon. We'll put off going to Mama's and we'll go out to dine, just the two of us.' He put up a hand and touched her cheek. 'You're a dear, old-fashioned girl, aren't you? You need to be wooed slowly; I should have known that.'

He was as good as his word. He came to take her out the following evening and by the end of it Lucy had almost made up her mind to leave the hospital at once and marry him just as soon as he wanted her to. They had dined at a quiet, luxurious hotel and danced for a while afterwards, and she couldn't help but be flattered by the attention they received. Fraam was obviously a well-known client and although he took it all for granted, she was made a little shy by it. They had walked back through the quiet, cold streets afterwards, and when they had got back into the house she had actually been on the point of telling him that she would do as he wished, but the telephone had rung and when he had gone to answer it, he had bidden her a hurried goodnight and left the house.

She saw him at breakfast, but as he was on the point of going as she reached the table, there was no time for more than a quick kiss and an assurance that he would be home for lunch.

As indeed he was, but with a guest. 'Adilia,' he introduced her coolly, and Lucy, instantly disliking her, greeted her with a sweetness only matched by her new acquaintance.

'We met outside and since Adilia tells me that she is at a loose end I invited her for lunch.' He added carelessly: 'I told Jaap as we came in. And what have you two been doing with your morning?'

He sat down between Lisabertha and Adilia, opposite Lucy, and it was to her he looked. Lucy began some sort of a reply, to be interrupted gently by Adilia, who demanded, in the prettiest way imaginable, that she might be given a drink. And after that she kept the conversation in her own hands, and during

lunch as well, even though Lisabertha did her best to
start up a more general conversation so that Lucy
might join in; for how could she do that when the
talk was of people she didn't know and times when
she hadn't even known Fraam. She looked composed
enough, made polite rejoinders when she was addressed and seethed inside her. Adilia might only be
a girl Fraam had known for years, but she was a
beautiful one and she had a lovely voice, a low laugh
and the kind of clothes Lucy had hankered after for
years. She decided that the wisest course was to at-
tempt no competition at all and was pleased to see
presently that Adilia found it disconcerting. All the
same they parted on the friendliest of terms, and
Lucy, talking animatedly, managed to avoid Fraam,
calling a casual goodbye as he went through the door
with Adilia, who had begged a lift, beside him.

'You do not like her,' declared Lisabertha instantly, leading the way back to the sitting room.

'I can't say I do,' agreed Lucy, 'though I daresay
I'm jealous of her; she's quite beautiful and she
wears gorgeous clothes.'

'And you also will wear such clothes when you
are Fraam's wife, and you may not be a beauty, but
he has chosen you, has he not?'

Lucy said 'Yes' doubtfully and because she didn't
want to talk about it, said that she had letters to write
and had better get them done and posted.

And that evening, when Fraam came home and

they were having drinks before dinner, he asked her what she had thought of Adilia. It would have been nice to have told him what she did think, but instead she said rather colourlessly that Adilia was beautiful. He laughed then and added: 'So now you know what she's like, my dear.'

CHAPTER NINE

LUCY HAD SPENT an almost sleepless night wondering exactly what Fraam had meant. He hadn't said
any more; dinner had been a pleasant affair, just the
three of them, and the talk had been of the family
dinner party at their mother's house the next evening.
'Have you got that green dress with you?' Fraam
wanted to know, and when Lucy answered a surprised yes: 'Then wear it, my dear, it suits you very
well.' He had smiled to send her heart dancing:
'There will be more family for you to meet; there
are a great many of us...'

'Aunts and uncles,' chimed in Lisabertha, 'and
cousins. I suppose that horrid Tante Sophie will be
there.'

'Naturally, and you will be nice to her, Lisa, although I think that we must all take care that Lucy
doesn't fall into her clutches.'

'Why not?' asked Lucy.

'She is malicious. Perhaps she does not mean to
be, but she can be unkind.'

'Well, if I don't understand her...'

'She speaks excellent English. But don't worry,
we'll not give her a chance to get you alone.'

All the same, Lucy found herself alone with the lady the next evening. Dinner was over, a splendid, leisurely meal, shared by some twenty people and all of them, it seemed, der Linssens. They had had their coffee in the drawing room and had broken up into small groups the better to talk, and someone or other had delayed Fraam as they had been crossing the room, and Lucy found herself alone. But only for a moment. Tante Sophie had appeared beside her and no one had noticed her taking Lucy by the arm and leading her on to the covered balcony adjoining the drawing room.

'I'm really waiting for Fraam,' began Lucy. 'He's just stopped to speak to someone…'

'He will find us here,' beamed Tante Sophie. 'I have been so anxious to have you to myself for just a few minutes, Lucy. Such a sweet girl you are, you will make an excellent wife for Fraam; so quiet and malleable and never questioning.'

'Why should I question him?' asked Lucy curiously.

Tante Sophie looked arch. 'My dear, surely you know that Fraam is what you call a lady's man? That is an old-fashioned term, is it not, but I am sure that you understand it. So many pretty girls…' she sighed, 'the fortunate man, he could have taken his pick of any one of them, but he chose you. You haven't known him long?' Her voice had grown a little sharp.

Lucy didn't answer. She wondered if it would be very rude if she just walked away, but Tante Sophie still had a beringed hand on her arm.

'Of course, my dear Lucy, we older ones find it difficult to understand you young people—not that Fraam is a young man…' Lucy opened her mouth to make an indignant protest, but she had no chance. 'You are permissive, is that not the right word? Why, I could tell you tales—but wives turn a blind eye these days, it seems, just as you will learn to do.'

Tante Sophie had small, beady black eyes. Like a snake, thought Lucy, staring at her and trying to think of something to say. The lady was so obviously wanting her to ask all the questions she was just as obviously wanting to answer. When she didn't speak Tante Sophie said tartly: 'Well, it is to be hoped that he won't break your heart; he's never loved a girl for more than a few days.'

Lucy felt Fraam's large hand on her shoulder. Its pressure was reassuring and very comforting. 'He's never loved a girl,' he corrected the old lady blandly, 'until now. Have you been trying to frighten Lucy, Tante Sophie?' His voice was light, but Lucy could feel his anger.

'Of course not!' The elderly voice was shrill with spite. 'Well, I must go and talk to your mother, Fraam.' Her peevish gaze swept the room behind them. 'Such a pity it is just family. A few of those lovely girls of yours would have made the evening a good deal livelier.'

They watched her go, and Fraam's hand slipped from Lucy's shoulder to her waist. 'Sorry about that,' he observed easily. 'Do you want to call our engagement off?'

He was laughing as he spoke and she laughed back at him. Now he was there beside her, all the silly little doubts Tante Sophie's barbed remarks had raised were quieted. 'Of course not! She must be very unhappy to talk like that.'

'Clever girl to see that. Yes, she is, that's why we all bear with her.' He smiled down at her and for a moment Lucy thought that he was going to kiss her. But he didn't—perhaps, she told herself sensibly, because someone might turn round and see them, but it didn't matter; he loved her and everything was all right.

All right until lunch time the next day. She and Lisabertha had been out shopping and while they were waiting to cross the busy street at the Munt, she saw the unmistakable Panther de Ville coming towards them. And Adilia was sitting beside Fraam. Lucy watched it pass them in silence and it was Lisabertha who exclaimed: 'Well, what on earth is she doing with Fraam? He told me he was working until at least three o'clock.'

'Perhaps he finished early,' Lucy heard her voice, carefully colourless, utter the trite words, and her companion hastened to agree with her. But Lucy didn't really listen; she was thinking about Adilia. In the few seconds during which the car had passed, Lucy had had the general impression of loveliness and chic and beautiful clothes, and an even stronger impression that Adilia had seen her...

By the time they got home she was in a splendid turmoil of temper, hurt, and doubt. She could hardly wait until Fraam returned so that she might unburden herself; men who were just engaged didn't go riding round the city with other girls, nor did they tell lies about working until three o'clock when they weren't. When he did get home she was sitting in the drawing room alone, for Lisabertha, sensing her mood, had retired discreetly to her room. Fraam barely had time to close the door behind him when she told him icily: 'I saw you this afternoon—at lunchtime—with Adilia. You said you would be working until three o'clock.' She added waspishly: 'I suppose you took her out to lunch.'

His expression didn't change at all and she couldn't see the gleam in his eyes. 'Er—no, my dear.' She waited for him to say something more than that and when he didn't she got up and started for the door. She knew that she was behaving childishly and that she would probably burst into tears in no time at all; she had been spoiling for a nice down-to-earth quarrel and Fraam had no intention of quarrelling. Was this what Tante Sophie had meant? Was this learning to turn a blind eye? A sob bubbled up in her throat and escaped just as she had a hand on the door, but she never opened it. Fraam had got there too and turned her round and caught her close.

'Now, now, my love,' he said soothingly, 'what's all this?' He kissed the top of her head. 'I believe Tante Sophie's hints and spite did their work, after all.' He turned her face up to his and carefully wiped away a tear. 'I told you I would be working until three o'clock, but what I didn't explain was that I had a list at another hospital. I was driving there when Adilia stopped me and asked for a lift. And I didn't have lunch with her—indeed, I haven't had lunch at all.'

'Oh, aren't I awful?' Lucy said woefully, 'jumping to conclusions, and you going without your lunch. I feel mean and a bit silly.'

'You're not mean and you're not silly, but supposing we get married as soon as we can, then you'll be quite sure of me, won't you?'

'You mean I'm not quite sure of you now?' she asked him quickly. 'Well, no, perhaps I'm not. But don't you see, while I'm not then how can I marry you?' She went on earnestly: 'I think I should go back to St Norbert's and—and not see you for a bit and then you'll be sure...'

'Sure of what?' His voice was very quiet.

'Well, wanting to marry me.'

'And you? Would you be sure then, Lucy?'

She looked at him in surprise. 'Me? Oh, but I'm sure—I mean, sure that I love you.'

'So it is for me that you wish to go back to hospital? Not for yourself?'

She nodded. 'Yes. You do have to be quite certain.'

'And you think that I am not. Shall I tell you something, Lucy? The world is full of Adilias, but there is only one Lucy.' He pulled her to him and kissed her slowly. 'I can't teach you to trust me; that's something you must do for yourself, and I think that you do trust me, only you have this ridiculous idea that every girl in the world is beautiful except you, and because of that you have this chip on your shoulder which prevents you from accepting the fact that anyone could possibly want to marry you.'

'I have not got a chip on my shoulder,' said Lucy pettishly. 'I'm trying to be sensible.' She wanted to cry again, but she didn't know why.

'All right, no chip.' He kissed her again. 'We won't talk about it any more now; I have to go back to my rooms after tea, but after dinner this evening we'll talk again, and this time I shall persuade you to change your mind and marry me as soon as possible.'

She leaned her head against his shoulder and thought that probably she would be persuaded because that was what she wanted to do really. She said quite happily: 'Yes, all right—I like being with you and talking, Fraam.'

They had tea together presently, and Lucy had felt utterly content. This was going to be marriage with Fraam; quiet half hours in which to talk and knowing that he would be home again in the evening. Just the sight of him sitting opposite her, drinking his tea and eating cake and telling her about his day at the hospital, made her feel slightly giddy with happiness. Her matter-of-fact acceptance of her plain face was being edged away by a new-found assurance stemming from that same happiness and after all not many girls had green eyes. When Fraam had gone she went upstairs and washed her hair and wound it painstakingly into rollers while she did her face. The results were not startling but at least they were an improvement. She would buy a new dress or two, she thought happily, and when later that evening they would have their talk, she would agree to anything he said. He had been right, of course; the reason why she wasn't quite sure of him was because she hadn't quite believed that he could prefer her to other girls. She skipped downstairs to wait for him.

He didn't come. There was a telephone message a little later to say that there had been an accident—one of the surgeons on duty—and Fraam would stay in his place until he could be relieved. The two girls dined alone and the evening passed pleasantly enough discussing the clothes Lucy would like to buy. 'Get all you want,' advised Lisabertha. 'Fraam has a great deal of money and he will pay the bills.'

'I'd rather not—at least, not until he suggests it, if he ever does. I've some money, enough to buy a dress.'

They went to bed presently and Lucy, thinking of Fraam, slept dreamlessly.

He was at breakfast the next morning, immersed in his letters, making notes in his pocketbook and scanning the newspaper headlines. He got up when she joined him, settled her in a chair beside him, declared in a rather absentminded way that she looked as pretty as a picture, kissed her briefly and went on: 'I have to go to Brussels this morning—there's a patient there I've looked after for some time and his own doctor wants me there for a consultation. I'm flying down, Jaap will take me to Schiphol, and I should be back this evening—wait up for me, Lucy, there is something I want to tell you.'

'Can't you tell me now?' She tried not to sound anxious. His 'no' was very decisive.

Lucy was alone in the sitting room after lunch when Jaap came into the room.

'There is a visitor for you, Miss Prendergast,' he announced uneasily.

Adilia looked lovely, but then she always did. She brushed past Jaap as though he weren't there and addressed Lucy. 'I've come to fetch some things I forgot to take with me.'

Lucy felt puzzled. 'Things?' she asked, and added politely: 'Well, I'm sure Fraam won't mind if you collect them—where did you leave them?'

Adilia gave her a wicked look. 'Upstairs, of course—where else do you suppose? In the Brocade Room.' She gave a little laugh. 'Fraam called you the parson's daughter, and you really are, aren't you?'

She sank down into one of the large winged chairs, apparently in no hurry, arranging herself comfortably before she observed: 'Why do you suppose Fraam is marrying you, Lucy? He needs a wife...' she glanced round the beautiful room, 'someone to run his household and rear his children. That's not for me,' she shrugged briefly. 'I'm all for freedom, so he can't have me—not on a permanent basis—and now he doesn't care who he marries. You will do as well as any, I daresay—probably better.'

Lucy felt cold inside and there was a peculiar sensation in her head. All the same she said sturdily: 'I don't believe you.'

Adilia got up, stretched herself and yawned prettily. 'It's all the same to me. You will be an excellent wife, for you will never allow yourself to wonder if Fraam is really in Munich or Brussels at some seminar or other, or ask where he has been when he comes home late.' She nodded her beautiful head. 'It is a great advantage to be a parson's daughter—he sees that too.'

Lucy was on her feet now, her small capable hands clenched on either side of her. 'I still don't believe you,' she said, and somehow managed to keep her doubts out of her voice.

'You don't want to. Fraam is in Brussels, is he not, or so he told you.' Adilia tugged the bell rope and when Jaap came: 'Jaap, you drove Mr der Linssen to Schiphol, did you not? We are both so silly, we cannot remember where he was going.'

Jaap marshalled his English. 'To London, Juffrouw—the ten o'clock flight.'

Adilia nodded dismissal and he went away, looking puzzled and a little worried; Miss Prendergast had looked quite ill when he had said that...

'You see?' asked Adilia when the door had been closed. She crossed the room and tapped Lucy on the shoulder. 'Jaap does not lie—you have to believe him. And now you will have to believe me; I am going to London too.'

She went to the door. 'There is one thing of which you may be very sure: I am very discreet. But what should you care? You will have what you want—this house, Fraam's money and a clutch of children—they will be plain, just like you.'

She had gone, closing the door very quietly behind her, and Lucy stood speechless, the strength of her feelings tearing through her like a force ten gale. Rage and misery and humiliation all jostled for a place in her bewildered head and for the moment at any rate, rage won. She tore at the ring on her finger and then raced from the room, up the stairs and into her bedroom, there to fling on her coat, tie a scarf over her hair and snatch up her gloves. She was in the hall and almost at the door when Jaap came through the little arched door which led to the kitchens.

'You go out, miss?' he asked. He didn't allow his well-schooled features to lose their blandness, but his voice was anxious.

'Yes. Yes, Jaap.' She looked at him quite wildly, still re-living those terrible minutes with Adilia. 'I'm going away.' She darted past him, got the heavy door open and was away before he could stop her.

She had no idea where she was going, but she wasn't thinking about that. She had no idea in which direction she was walking either; she was running away, intent on putting as much distance between her and her hurt as possible. She hurried along, thinking how strange it was that she had been so happy and that just a few words from someone could sweep that happiness away like sand before the wind.

She walked on, right through the heart of the city, without being aware of it, and when the street she was in merged into the Mauritskade, she turned along it and then into Stadhouderskade and so into Leidsestraat. She trudged down that too, and if it hadn't begun to rain she might have gone on and on and ended up at Schiphol; as it was she turned round and started back again towards the centre of Amsterdam. She was tired now and she wasn't really thinking any more, aware only of a dull headache and an empty feeling deep inside her. It had grown from afternoon dusk to wintry evening and she realised that she was cold and hungry and needed to rest, and over and above that, it was impossible for her to go back to Fraam's house ever again. She would go home, of course, but just at the moment she was quite incapable of making any plans, first she must have a meal.

She had reached the inner ring of the *grachten* again and there were hotels on every side. She recognised one of them; Fraam had taken her there to dine only a short time ago. She went inside and booked a room at the reception desk, for she had to sleep somewhere and she remembered that he had told her that it was a respectable hotel. She didn't ask the price of the room; her head was still full of her own unhappy thoughts and she brushed aside the receptionist's polite enquiry as to luggage, following the bell boy into the lift like an automaton and when she was alone in the room, sitting down without even taking her coat off. But presently she bestirred herself and looked around her. The apartment was luxurious, more so than she had expected, and the adjoining bathroom was quite magnificent. She washed her white face and telephoned for a meal. It was while she was waiting for it that she realised that she had no money. And no passport either.

She ate her dinner when it came because whatever trouble lay ahead of her, and there would be trouble, it would be easier to face if she were nicely full; all the same, she had no idea what she ate.

When the room waiter had cleared away she undressed, had a bath and got into bed. She already owed for her dinner, she might as well owe for a night's rest as well. She really didn't care what they would do to her, although she wondered what the Dutch prisons were like. But her thoughts soon returned to Fraam. She would have to send him a message or write to him—probably from prison. She chuckled at the thought and the chuckle turned into tears until, quite worn out with her weeping, she slept.

She woke in the night, her mind clear and sensible; all she had to do was to telephone Jaap in the morning and ask him to send round her handbag. All the money she possessed was in it, and so was her passport. It was a pity she would have to leave her clothes behind, but they weren't important; she would be able to pay the bill and go to Schiphol and catch the first flight possible. She wondered if she had enough money; as far as she could remember there had been all of fifty pounds in her purse, surely more than sufficient. She closed her eyes and slept again.

It was after breakfast, taken in her room, and an

unsatisfactory toilet that she went down to the reception desk. There was another clerk on duty now, a sharp-faced woman who bade her a grudging good morning and asked her if she wanted her bill.

It seemed the right moment to explain. Lucy embarked on her story; she had left the house without her purse and could she telephone to have it sent to her at the hotel. It wasn't until she had come to the end of it that she saw that the clerk didn't believe a word of it. All the same she gave her the number. 'It's Mijnheer der Linssen's house,' she explained. 'He is known here, isn't he?' And when the woman nodded grudgingly: 'Well, I'm his fiancée.' Too late she saw the woman's eyes fly to her ringless hands. She had plucked off her lovely ring and left it…where had she left it? She had no idea.

'I'll call the manager,' said the clerk, still polite but hostile. And when he came, elegant and courteous, the whole story was repeated, but this time in Dutch and by the clerk, so that Lucy couldn't understand a word. At the end of it the manager spoke pleasantly enough. 'By all means make your call, Miss…' he refreshed his memory from the register before him, 'Miss Prendergast. Perhaps you wouldn't mind waiting in your room afterwards?' He smiled. 'Your handbag shall be brought to you there.'

Lucy sighed with relief and went to one of the telephone booths. Jaap sounded upset, but she didn't give him a chance to speak. 'My handbag,' she urged him, 'it's on the dressing table in my room, please will you send it round as soon as you can? You do understand?' She heard him draw breath and his hurried 'Yes, miss,' but didn't give him a chance to say anything else. 'And Jaap, don't tell anyone I'm here—not anyone. Here's the address, and do please hurry. And thank you, Jaap.'

She went upstairs at once since the manager had been so insistent; perhaps they thought it would be easier and save time if they knew where she was. It was a little irksome to stay there, though, for the urge to get away was getting stronger every minute. An hour passed and she became more and more uneasy; she didn't think that it would take all that time to come from Fraam's house, she decided to go down to the desk and see if it had been delivered and forgotten.

She had been locked in. She stared at the door in disbelief and tried the handle again, fruitlessly, and when she lifted the receiver no one answered. Not a girl to panic, she went and sat down and tried to think calmly. In a way it was a relief to have something to worry about; it stopped her thinking about Fraam. She thought of him now of course and tears she really couldn't stop spilled from her tired eyes and ran down her unmade-up face. If he had been there, this would never have happened, she told herself with muddled logic. But he wasn't there, he was in London, possibly even now waiting eagerly at the airport for Adilia. The thought made the tears flow even faster and she uttered a small wail. The sound of the key turning in the lock sent her round facing the wall so that they shouldn't see her face. When the door was opened and shut again she cried in a soggy whisper: 'Oh, do please go away!' only to swing round at once, because of course if they went away she wouldn't get her bag...

Fraam was standing there with a white and furious face, her handbag in his hand. He said in a bitter voice she hardly recognised: 'You wanted this? Presumably you left home so fast that you forgot it.'

He looked enquiringly at her, his brows raised, but she didn't answer him.

'You should be more careful,' he told her. 'You need both money and passport when you run away.' His eyes swept over her tatty person. 'Make-up too, and a comb.'

Surprise had checked her tears, but at this remark they all came rushing back again. How dared he poke fun at her! She meant to tell him so, but all she said in a wispy voice was: 'They locked me in.'

His mouth twitched. 'And quite right too. They weren't to know whether you were lying or not, were they? And you were lying, Lucy. I found your ring in your teacup—an extraordinary place—so I must take it that you are no longer my fiancée.' He added sternly: 'There is a law against false pretences.'

It seemed to Lucy that she was getting nowhere at

all. She had the right to upbraid him, but she had had no chance. To point out his duplicity, confront him with his two-faced behaviour. Suddenly indignant, she took a deep breath and opened her mouth. She was dreadfully unhappy, but an angry outburst might help her to forget that.

'And before you launch your attack,' said Fraam in a surprisingly mild voice now, 'I want an explanation.'

She choked on the words she had been preparing to utter. 'You want an explanation? It's me that wants one!' Her voice rose to a watery squeak. 'Adilia said…'

'Ah, now we are getting to the heart of the matter, the—er—nigger in the woodpile.'

Her rage had gone, there was nothing but a cold unhappy lump in her chest.

'Don't joke, Fraam—please don't joke,' and when she saw how good-humoured he was looking now, she added pettishly: 'Why do you look so pleased with yourself? Just now when you came in you were furiously angry.'

He was leaning against the wall, his hands in his pockets, looking, she was shocked to see, as though he was enjoying himself. 'My dear girl, no man worth his salt likes to find his fiancée—ex-fiancée— locked in an hotel bedroom because she can't pay the bill. Over and above that, I was roused from a night's sleep by Jaap's agitated request that I should catch the next plane and return home because you had left the house rather more hastily than he liked. I've had no breakfast and I'm tired, and until a few minutes ago, the most terrified man on earth. And now tell me what Adilia said to cause you to tear away in such a fashion.'

'You went to London,' Lucy pointed out in a wobbly voice, 'and you told me you were going to Brussels, and Adilia said—she said that she was going to London too and that I was a parson's daughter and you only wanted to marry me because she wouldn't have you.' She sucked in a breath like a tearful child. 'And she said I'd have p-plain children, just like me.'

A spasm passed over Fraam's handsome features. He dealt with what was obvious to him to be the most hurtful of these remarks. 'Little girls with green eyes and soft mouths are the most beautiful of God's creatures,' he said in a gentle voice, 'and as for the boys, they will be our sons, Lucy, with, I hope, their mother's sweet nature and my muscle.'

He left the wall so suddenly that the next thing she knew she was wrapped in his arms. 'You silly, silly little girl,' he observed, 'did you not know that I would come after you wherever you went?'

Lucy sniffed. It was very satisfying to feel his tight hold, but they still hadn't dealt with the crux of the matter. 'Adilia said...' she began, and was interrupted by Fraam's forceful: 'Damn Adilia, but since you have to get her off your chest, my darling, let us hear what the woman said and be done with it.'

It was a little difficult to begin. Lucy muttered and mumbled a good deal, but once she got started the words poured out in a jumble which hardly made sense. But Fraam listened patiently and when she paused at last, not at all sure that she had made herself clear, he had the salient points at his fingertips. 'Dear heart, will you believe me when I say that Adilia has never, at any time, stayed at my house? There was nothing of hers in the Brocade Room or anywhere else in my home. Why should there be? You have been the only girl, Lucy. She was making mischief—people do, you know; they're bored with their own lives and it amuses them to upset those of other people.'

'Of course I believe you,' declared Lucy, and added after a moment's thought: 'You went to London—she asked Jaap, you know, and he told us. Because I didn't believe her.'

'I went to London, my dearest darling, to see the Senior Nursing Officer of St Norbert's, for it had become increasingly clear to me that getting married to you was more important than anything else and all this hanging around for a month until you could leave was quite unnecessary. I saw your father briefly too and asked him about a licence. If you would agree, we could be married within the week.'

'But you didn't say a word...'

'I was afraid you would have all kinds of arguments against it, my love.' He kissed the top of her head. 'No time to buy clothes, you would have said, certainly no time to arrange for bridesmaids, no time to send out invitations…'

Lucy considered. 'I don't mind about any of those things,' she told him, 'though of course I must buy a dress…'

'My dear sensible girl, and so beautiful too.' And when she looked at him she saw that he meant it. 'At your home? And your father, of course. My family can fly over,' his eyes narrowed in thought, 'I'll charter a plane.'

'But that's extravagant!'

'Surely one may be forgiven a little extravagance at such a time, my darling.' He loosed her for a moment, found her ring in a pocket and slipped it on her finger. 'Why a teacup?' he wanted to know.

'I don't know—I don't remember, I was so unhappy.'

'You shall never be unhappy again, dear heart.' He kissed her slowly. 'And now we're going home.'

Lucy received the manager's apology with a smile. She was so happy herself that she wanted everyone else to be the same, only she longed to wave her hand with the ring once more upon it under the clerk's nose.

They hardly spoke as Fraam drove through the city. It wasn't until they were in the hall with a beaming Jaap shutting the door on the outside world that Lucy spoke.

'Fraam, were you ever in love with Adilia, or—or any of those girls you danced with at the hospital ball?'

He turned her round to face him, holding her gently by the shoulders.

'No, my love, just amusing myself while I was waiting for you to come along, and when you did I was so afraid that you would have none of me...I think I am still a little afraid of that.'

Lucy flung her arms round his neck. 'The first time you saw me—at that lecture, you looked as though you wanted to shake me.'

'Did I? I wanted to get off that platform and carry you off and marry you out of hand...I fell in love with you then, my darling.'

She leaned back the better to see his face. 'Did you really? And I looked such a mess!'

His hands were gentle on her. 'You looked beautiful, my darling, just as you look beautiful now.'

She leaned up and kissed him. 'That's such a satisfactory thing to have said of one,' she commented. 'I'm not sure that it's quite true, but oh, Fraam, I'm so glad I'm me!'

Jaap, coming from the dining room, looked carefully into the middle distance and coughed. 'There is breakfast,' he mentioned with dignity.

They both turned to look at him. 'Jaap, old friend,

you think of everything,' remarked Fraam as Lucy left him to take Jaap's hand.

'Thank you,' she said. 'I hope you'll be my old friend too.'

Jaap beamed once more. 'It will be my pleasure, Miss Prendergast.'

He watched the pair of them go into the dining room and then closed the door. On his way to the kitchen he ruminated happily on the days ahead. Such a lot to do; a wedding was always a nice thing to have in a family. He nodded his elderly head with deep satisfaction.

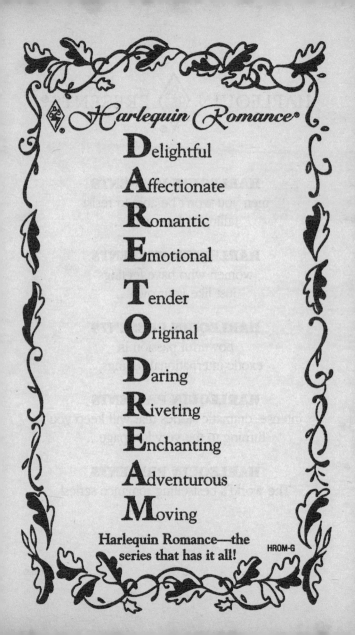

Harlequin Romance®

Delightful

Affectionate

Romantic

Emotional

Tender

Original

Daring

Riveting

Enchanting

Adventurous

Moving

Harlequin Romance—the
series that has it all!

HROM-G

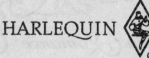

HARLEQUIN PRESENTS®

HARLEQUIN PRESENTS
men you won't be able to resist
falling in love with...

HARLEQUIN PRESENTS
women who have feelings
just like your own...

HARLEQUIN PRESENTS
powerful passion in
exotic international settings...

HARLEQUIN PRESENTS
intense, dramatic stories that will keep you
turning to the very last page...

HARLEQUIN PRESENTS
The world's bestselling romance series!